I0699948

TRACKER

TAM DeRUDDER JACKSON

A skilled warrior with a life-changing task…

Every warrior needs a talisman – but for Riley Sheridan, he cares more about partying with his buddies than finding the mate he's supposed to bond with for life. That is, until a stunning raven-haired woman steps up to the keg and asks for a beer.

A fiery beauty with untapped powers…

Lynnette Montgomery came to the festival to relax, celebrate, and take her mind off her still-undiscovered magical powers. But after fate draws her to a suave and cocky warrior, she's shocked to realize that she's his fated talisman. But finding your mate is never supposed to be this easy.

And the wrath of a goddess bent on their demise.

Drawn by a ripple in the cosmos, the infamous goddess Morrigan sets her sights on the pair. She's dead-set on stopping the next Sheridan from bonding to his talisman – and when they retreat to a remote cabin to complete the ritual, she sees her chance to strike. After the goddess kidnaps Riley, Lynette is thrust into a deadly battle with a seemingly impossible goal: to save him from a fate worse than death.

Bursting with all the pulse-pounding action and rich world-building of a riveting fantasy adventure, this gripping prequel is a must-read for fans of Tam DeRudder Jackson's *Talisman Series*, or as a starting point for your adventure into a world of modern-day Celtic warriors.

What readers are saying about the *Talisman Series*

"Loved this book! Fantasy, danger, excitement, and legend all woven into an epic love story. Felt like I was right in the middle of the action! Tam DeRudder Jackson is my new favorite romance author."

–AMAZON REVIEW FOR *TALISMAN*

"The second installment of the Talisman series delivers again and shows us what we all want—to find love and our fated mate, even when it's in front of us the whole time!"

–MICHELE PACKARD, AUTHOR OF THE
MATTI BAKER SERIES FOR *WARRIOR*

"PROPHETESS is a quick read; a fast paced story that overlaps with the events of book two Warrior but focuses on the relationship between two people who thought love and fate had left them behind. The premise is entertaining … the romance is passionate; the characters are colorful and charismatic."

–SANDY SCHAIRER, REVIEWER

"I would definitely recommend this book to readers who enjoy suspenseful paranormal romance. The characters are dynamic, the story is layered, and the romance is fantastic! I love how this pair challenges each other and how seamlessly they work together. They're both pretty amazing, and they make a great team."

–JULIE PETITBON, REVIEWER FOR *ROGUE*

"Fireworks!

In this fourth book in the Talisman Series, Seamus Lochlann the happy-go-lucky playboy warrior takes center stage and meets his other half. Fallon Graham said no to a date with him, but fate will not be denied. A rainstorm in the middle of nowhere, they are thrown together. An evil vengeful goddess has set her sights on Seamus and will stop at nothing to acquire him. Previous characters and new show up to make things more intriguing. I love this series so much. It's unique and grabs you and won't let go. A beautiful and well-written spicy story full of action and Celtic lore. I've long been a fan of mythology, so it's right up my alley. . . I hope this series never ends."

—Patricia White, reviewer for *Bard*

"Absolutely brilliant and breathtaking. Druid leaves you at your seat's edge, panting to get to the end. Anyone who read Fallon's and Seamus's story knows that Tam DeRudder [Jackson] is a wonderful storyteller with a talent for the epic. Now reading Davy's and Sloane's story just reiterates this. I most definitely look forward to reading more works from this author."

—Adebola Adekunbi, reviewer

Books by Tam DeRudder Jackson

THE TALISMAN SERIES

Talisman
Warrior
Prophetess (novella)
Bard
Druid
Rogue (stand alone)

THE BALEFIRE SERIES

Play For Me
Sing For Me
Wild For Me
Hot For Me

TRACKER

For Lori DeRudder Hodges

*Thank you for championing me throughout
this whole writing adventure.
Love you lots, Toots.*

CHAPTER ONE

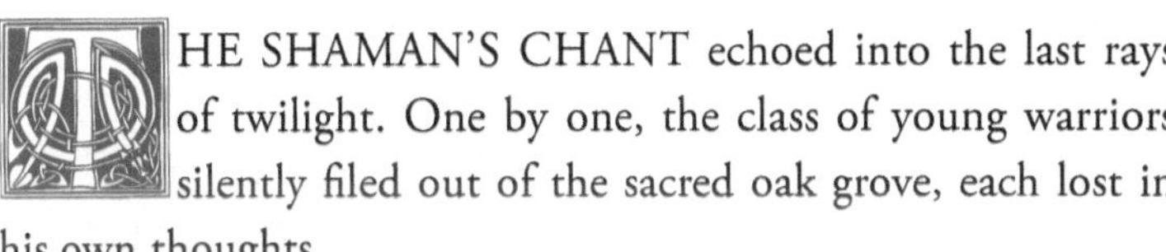

THE SHAMAN'S CHANT echoed into the last rays of twilight. One by one, the class of young warriors silently filed out of the sacred oak grove, each lost in his own thoughts.

At the edge of the shaman's property, Riley Sheridan, his fraternal twin Rio, and their friend Seamus Lochlann climbed into Riley's Jeep. For several long minutes, none of them said a word. At last, Seamus broke the silence. "That wasn't what I expected."

"Me neither," Riley said. "Why didn't Dad tell us we'd be lost in that weird dream world, desperate to find our way?"

In the passenger seat, Rio sat sideways, his ankle resting on his knee as he faced his brother. "That was your experience?"

"Yeah. Wasn't it yours?"

"Nope. I spent however long we were in there fighting zombie champions and wishing for Scathach to share a strategy with me." He glanced over his shoulder at Seamus in the back seat. "What happened to you?"

Their friend pulled a face. "I was parked on my ass in the tall grass waiting for someone to come along and talk to me."

Riley and Rio exchanged a grin.

"I know that shaman pulled herbs from the same satchel for each of us," Riley said. "I was watching. The chant sounded the same too. I mean, she might have hypnotized us or something with the way she droned on in Gaelic, but I'm pretty sure it was the same, so—"

"—why were our experiences so different?" his twin finished for him.

"Exactly."

"Probably for the same reason each of us was given a different sign to try on talismans in the community," Rio said.

From the back seat came, "Explain."

Rio shot Seamus a "duh" stare. "Each of us has a skill set that our fated mate will complement with her special skill. So it stands to reason we each have a different sign to try on talismans."

"Yeah, yeah, we all learned that in our earliest training. My question is, why were our experiences in that grove so different?" Seamus demanded.

A rite of passage, the sign ritual signaled the start of each warrior's quest to find and bond with his talisman—his fated mate. From tonight on, it was paramount that each warrior discover the woman who responded to his designated and quite personal sign. Having recently passed their twenty-first birthdays, each warrior who experienced the ritual now had seven years to complete that quest or face a life on the run or something worse—turning rogue and joining the Morrigan's evil minions to fight against warriors. Riley shuddered at the thought. Did their vastly different experiences mean something about who was going to find his mate on time—and who might not?

"Maybe it has to do with who our talismans are. Maybe it's a clue for where to look for them," Rio said.

Still feeling a bit groggy from whatever the shaman had done to them, Riley shrugged and fired up his Jeep. "If we drive all night, we should be home by midmorning tomorrow."

"That's another thing. Why did we have to take civilian transportation to this event?" Seamus groused. "Why couldn't we visualize ourselves here and pop back home when it was over? Because I sure could use a beer right about now."

Laughing, Riley put the Jeep in gear and backed out of the parking area in front of the classic red barn separating the sacred grove from the rest of the shaman's property.

Beside him, Rio pulled on his seat belt and glared at Seamus in the rearview mirror. "You never take anything seriously, do you? Finding and bonding with our fated mates is our highest priority now, and you're pissy because you can't party." He crossed his arms over his chest and stared straight ahead as Riley navigated the narrow two-track heading out to the main road.

Seamus sat forward in his seat. "How are you related to Riley again? Or Rowan for that matter? 'Cause both of them are fun."

Riley slid a glance his brother's way and saw him tense. For some reason no one had ever figured out, Rio had always been the most solemn Sheridan brother, relatively speaking. Growing up with the lot of them, it shouldn't have surprised Seamus that Rio would take the sign ritual—and its implications—so seriously.

Riley thought he heard Rio growl under his breath, "I am fun."

A smile tipped the corner of Riley's mouth. "How 'bout we find some food? A hamburger would be fun."

With a snort, Seamus sat back in his seat. From the corner of his eye, Riley caught Rio's sarcastic sneer as he reached over and turned up the tunes.

Even with Seamus's half-hearted whining and teasing, a quiet mood filled the vehicle. As his Jeep ate up the miles, Riley kept trying to figure out what kind of woman the gods had fated for him and why he'd experienced such a profound desperation to find his way in that tiny grove of trees. Glancing in the rearview, he saw Seamus staring out the side window, a contemplative expression on his face. He didn't need to slide a look in his twin's direction or try to breach his telepathic shield to know Rio was equally preoccupied with thoughts of his own experience and his lady too.

Turning twenty-one was a big deal in the civilian world—a rite of passage into the full privileges of adulthood that most civilians marked by partying in a bar until they puked. Warriors in their community, men and women of honor who were sworn to protect both the Celtic community and civilians alike, were expected to do their level best to find and bond with their talismans. Instead of celebrating adulthood, they were sworn to create strong fighting units that could take on the Morrigan and her evil armies and best them. Still, Seamus's idea of enjoying a beer after what they'd experienced sounded better and better as they drove through the night on their long diagonal trip from Southeast Montana to their home on Flathead Lake.

"Damn good thing the interstate took us through Billings. I doubt we'd find another all-night diner before my stomach turned inside out," Seamus said, as he climbed into the passenger seat of Riley's Jeep.

Rio was taking over this leg of the drive, so Riley slid into the backseat, prepared to nap off his massive midnight breakfast of waffles, sausages, a three-egg omelet, hash browns, a carafe of orange juice—and a hamburger. It had been a long time since they'd last eaten, having been warned to enter the sacred grove with an empty stomach. By the time the ritual had ended, nothing in the tiny towns they'd rolled through on their way north was open until they reached a decent-sized city. Casinos, bless 'em, served food all night.

Riley rolled up his protective leather jacket and stuffed it between the seat back and the window, preparing to sleep when Rio let out a low whistle and Seamus braced his hands on the dashboard.

"That didn't take long." Sarcasm coated Rio's quiet comment.

"The old girl is impatient. I would have thought she'd wait till one of us needed to take a leak somewhere on the side of the road out in the middle of nowhere," Seamus said as he unbuckled the seatbelt he'd just clicked into place.

Riley sat up and glanced out the windshield to see a group of five or six men moving toward them, the bright lights of the Jeep glinting off the claymores they held.

"Well, at least we get to do this on a full stomach," Seamus quipped as he pulled the handle on the door and stepped out.

From beneath his brows, Riley glared at the scene in front of them and slid into his leather jacket before he too climbed out of the Jeep. Rio stuffed the keys in his jeans pocket as he joined his brother and their friend outside their ride.

As one, the three warriors called their claymores to their hands and casually walked in front of the Jeep to face the rogues who had stopped several paces in front of them.

One rogue stepped forward. His eyes glowed an otherworldly red, marking him as one of the Morrigan's minions. "It appears we outnumber you two to one, gentlemen. Care to wager how this is going to go?"

As usual whenever their older brother Rowan or their dad wasn't with them, Rio took the lead, his voice deceptively calm. "Six dead rogues and three warriors back on the road home."

"Cocky much, Rio Sheridan?"

At hearing his brother's name, Riley gripped his claymore a bit tighter. This wasn't an accidental meeting. Morgan sent these guys with a singular goal. Jesus, he truly despised the old witch and her insatiable need to attack him and his family.

"Nope. Just stating facts."

As the two exchanged pleasantries, the other rogues fanned out in a semi-circle, effectively corralling him and his brother and Seamus between them and his Jeep. From the corner of his eye, he caught the feral grin spreading across Rio's face and hoped Seamus saw it too. Opening his telepathic shield to his friends, Riley heard Rio in his head. "On three we land behind them. One. Two. Three."

In a blink, the three of them had bent time and space to land on the balls of their feet with the tips of their claymores prodding the spines of the three rogues who stood in front of the Jeep, including the leader. "About that wager," Rio hissed right as the rogue spun and engaged Rio's sword, signaling the fight was on.

Without their talismans, the warriors and rogues were somewhat evenly matched. If they'd had their talismans, the women could have directed them, seen the battle in prophecy or real time, given them orders and commands for how to best the rogues most easily, and the three of them would have had the upper hand. As it was, they were on their own in hand-to-hand combat with men who lacked ethics and who, like their mistress, never played fair.

Their only ace in the hole was that unlike the rogues, the three of them trained with Scathach, the warrior trainer herself. She'd been drilling them on some moves that used pirouettes more than thrust and parry. Muscle memory kicked in, and Riley put those moves to use, taking out the rogue he'd engaged at about the same time Rio finished off his adversary. Beside them, Seamus was battling two rogues at once, with a third seeming to materialize out of nowhere.

Riley jumped over the downed rogue in front of him and with a bloodcurdling yell, drew the attention of that third rogue. Like a cartoon character, the man's eyes popped wide open before he dropped into a ready stance. Riley came at him with his claymore spinning, a blurry flash in the streetlights illuminating the parking lot. The rogue tried to focus on some part of him, but this was the first move Riley's father had taught him back when he still jumped in mud puddles and practiced with a wooden sword. Before the man could find his shot, Riley had caught his claymore and spun it out across the pavement. Terror rippled over the man's features, but he was done before he managed the first step toward his weapon. A scream from somewhere to his right alerted him that Rio or Seamus had had similar success.

Another sound penetrated his brain, and he exchanged glances with his buddies. They didn't need telepathy to know now was a good time to hit the road. Without a word, they climbed into the Jeep and Rio fired it up, careful to back away slowly so as to leave as little trace of their presence as possible. The sound of civilian police sirens crescendoed from the north end of the parking lot nearest the main road, so Rio spun the wheel toward the opposite exit, taking his time leaving the scene. The scenic route behind the casino took them through a quiet residential area. Rio slowly navigated through several blocks before finding a main artery in the city, one that would take them back to the interstate where they could safely use speed to escape.

From the passenger seat, Seamus snorted. "That's it right there."

"What?" Riley asked.

"The reason we should have been allowed to visualize ourselves to that ritual," he grumbled as he stared out at the passing darkness. "I bet we aren't the only warriors Morgan sicced her minions on tonight." He crossed his arms over his chest.

"There's something sick and sadistic about trying to take warriors who only hours ago were given their ticket to freedom and a chance at a life with a wife and a family," Rio echoed from the driver's seat.

"Yet, here we are, and none of us was surprised." Riley angled himself into the corner between the door and the backrest where he could stretch out along the entire backseat. He grabbed his ball cap off the floor where it landed when he'd jerked his jacket back on and pulled it low over his eyes.

"Hope the old witch at least came in and cleaned up the mess before those civilian cops arrived," Seamus said. "'Cause even with the careful way you drove us out of there, Rio, obviously, someone called that event in, someone who saw the Jeep and could probably describe it."

"Morgan won't be able to help herself. She loves wading in the blood of battle too much to let those boys be discovered by civilian police," Rio said. The driving bass of a rap tune thumped through the cab of the Jeep. "You want to find us a different radio station? Something that doesn't make me want to turn this ride around and go back and confront that witchy goddess?"

Seamus scrolled the dial until he found a country station and left it there. In the light of a passing car, Riley saw Rio nod, and he let himself relax. When he woke up, a rosy glow on the western horizon told him they were about two-thirds of the way home. In the front seat, Seamus snorted and rearranged himself where he'd laid the seat back almost over Riley's legs. Rap played low on the radio again.

Sitting up, he rolled his shoulders and turned his head from side to side, working the kinks out from sleeping for six hours in the backseat of his ride. "I need to take a leak. Are we near a town or something? Maybe we can stop for breakfast."

"We'll hit the truck stop outside Missoula in about ten." Rio smirked into the rearview mirror. "Can you wait that long?"

Riley flipped him the bird and he laughed. A long snore interrupted them before Seamus shot forward in his seat. The only thing keeping him from bumping his head on the roof was his seat belt.

"What the hell? Where are we?"

"Good morning to you too, Sunshine," Rio said.

Seamus scrubbed a hand over his face. "Sorry. I thought Maeve was here. She and her evil twin surrounded us with about a hundred rogues." He leaned down and adjusted his seat back to an upright position. "Nightmare or something."

"Maeve, huh? That's interesting. Macha kept showing her face to me all night." Riley stared out the windshield. "Wonder what that's about."

"Guess I'm glad I didn't take a nap," Rio said. "Maybe I'll go on and drive the last two hours home after breakfast."

"Chicken." Riley chucked him on the shoulder. "You're going to have to sleep sometime."

"Yeah, but maybe by the time I do, the herbs that shaman used will have worn off and I won't be trying to jump out of my skin when I wake up." He slid a smirk Seamus's way, and their friend shook his head and sneered.

"Hilarious, Rio."

The weird night left its mark, though, and the three of them surreptitiously checked out the parking lot of the truck stop after Rio parked the Jeep on the edge of it where they could make a quick exit if they needed to. Inside, it was quiet with only a couple occupied tables. They chose one by the windows and ordered a mountain of food the waitress needed help to serve. They plowed through their meal without conversation, left a hefty tip, and exited the restaurant the same way they'd entered it—with their eyes wide open for any signs of the Morrigan or her rogues. But all was still.

Riley drove the last leg home, but in the passenger seat, Rio didn't relax.

CHAPTER TWO

Two months later

LYNNETTE MONTGOMERY FINISHED stocking the last shelf for the night. "You're going to the Lammas Day bonfire with me, right, Delaney?" Her best friend, Delaney Ferrell, was busy turning the sign to Closed in the front window of the convenience store and locking the front door. "It's been so hot, it'll be nice to hang out by the lake, drink a few beers, maybe meet someone fun."

"You know another group of warriors went through the signing ritual on summer solstice. No doubt there will be a ton of guys our age trying their signs like it's their job," Delaney said, her eyes dancing.

"Well, it kinda is their job," Lynnette said as she stretched her back and picked up the cardboard box at her feet. Automatically, she began breaking it down as she headed to the back of the store, Delaney on her heels.

As Lynnette slid the cardboard into the bin, her friend leaned against the storeroom door. "What do you suppose your warrior will be like?"

"Hot, I hope!"

Both women laughed.

"How 'bout you? What are you hoping for?"

Delaney's expression turned pensive. "Someone with ethics"—she softened her words with a wry twist of her lips—"and who can keep up with me on a battlefield."

Lynnette sighed. "It's kinda unfair how you already know your skill without even bonding with a warrior." She slipped past her friend and headed for the break room to retrieve her purse and car keys.

"For a while there, my parents were convinced I was a warrior too, like Teague." When she mentioned her brother, she rolled her eyes. "But we both know how much I like men."

Lynnette smirked. "Yeah, if being boy crazy were a sport, you'd have been a state champ in high school."

Delaney laughed. "My first two years of college too, I imagine."

They headed out the back of the store and Lynnette locked up and set the alarm on the door.

"I noticed you slowed down some this last year. I didn't want to mention it, but since you brought it up. . ."

Her friend shrugged. "I dunno. After I turned twenty-one in January, it occurred to me I should probably stop chasing civilian men who would never understand why I went from 'Oh, baby, you're so fun' to 'I'm in a serious life-long relationship now' in the blink of an eye."

Lynnette raised a brow.

"You know. When my warrior finds me."

With a sage nod, Lynnette said, "Makes sense. It was just abrupt, like you flipped a switch." She hit her key fob and unlocked the doors on her utilitarian compact car.

Delaney slid into the passenger seat. "Scathach might have mentioned something."

In the interior light of the car, merriment danced on Lynnette's face as pink tinged her friend's cheeks. "Ah. That makes so much more sense. Scathach doesn't want any of her warriors distracted by silly little things like *feelings*."

Delaney snorted out a laugh. "Exactly."

As they rolled along the short main street of the tiny northwest Montana logging community they called home, Lynnette asked again, "But you are coming out to the lake with me tonight, aren't you? Even if you're not boy crazy anymore, you can be my wingwoman."

"Right," came her friend's dry response. "What happens if one of those warriors you expect to be there turns out to be my fated mate?"

"Then you can thank me after for insisting you tag along."

"This is why we'll always be besties." Delaney grinned as Lynnette drove up the long dirt road to the Ferrell family compound at the base of the mountain.

The rich smell of wood smoke drifted to her nose as Lynnette stepped out of her car in the parking area of the campground. It had taken her a minute to find the right spot on the opposite side of Swann Lake from the highway. In the thick forest surrounding the lake, twilight fell early, and she'd missed the turn the first time, so she had to backtrack. As she rounded the front of her car, a weird sensation rippled through her. Never in her life had she lost her way even for a minute, so how had she missed that turn?

"Hey, you want to hold on to these for me?" She handed her car keys to her friend.

Delaney shot her a look. "After our conversation this afternoon, now *you're* the one looking to get lucky tonight?" But she pocketed Lynnette's keys anyway.

"Not really. I had a weird premonition is all." She shrugged. "It's probably nothing."

Raucous laughter greeted them as they neared the bonfire burning brightly on the lakeshore, its flames reflected in the dark, still water. People sat on logs several feet away from the heat, drinking and talking. A group of guys stood near the picnic table, one of them pumping air into a pony keg on ice while another one filled Solo cups and handed them around. Bags of chips and other assorted snacks were stacked on the table, and Lynnette wandered over to it to add their contribution of a couple of party-size jars of peanuts she'd grabbed from work.

As they neared the table, a low whistle greeted them. "Hell-o ladies," said a hot blond who was built like a linebacker. "Want a beer?"

"Sure," she and Delaney said in unison. For a second, they stared at each other and bright smiles broke over their faces.

"You don't look like a matched pair, but you kinda sound like one," the blond said. "I'm Seamus."

"Nice to meet you, Seamus," Lynnette said as she accepted a beer from the guy handing them out. His midnight blue eyes twinkled, and she thought he looked a little older than the rest of the group.

"So, we could—and probably will—call you Gorgeous"—he let his eyes slide over her—"and Beautiful"—he gave Delaney the same attention—"but your names would be good too." Over the rim of his cup, he winked at her and downed some beer.

"I'm Lynnette, and this is my friend Delaney."

"You live around here?" asked the hot guy to his right.

For a minute, all Lynnette could do was stare. While Seamus was good looking in an all-American football player kind of way, the man next to him was quite possibly the most handsome man she'd ever seen. He easily topped six feet with broad shoulders that tapered to a taut waist and trim hips. The tight blue T-shirt he'd tucked into his jeans read "Byte Me" in blocky neon-green letters. He didn't bother with a belt. The light of the campfire danced in the black depths of his hair. Standing across from him, she couldn't discern the color of his eyes, but something about him reminded her of the guy manning the keg, so she wondered if they were some shade of blue too.

Beside her, Delaney hissed, "Stop staring and introduce yourself."

Instead, she swallowed a sip of nasty keg beer in an attempt to drown the butterflies threatening to fly out of her stomach.

Delaney huffed a sigh at her and turned to Mr. Hottie. "Yeah. We live across the lake. Where are you guys from?"

"All the little towns along Flathead," Seamus said.

"All at once?" Delaney flirted back. "Impressive."

In the firelight, Hottie's eyes twinkled as he stared back at Lynnette. "I'm Riley. And that guy"—with his thumb, he indicated the man pumping the keg—"is my twin, Rio. Nice to meet you." He saluted them with his beer.

The dancing light of the fire precluded her from discerning if any of the men had the telltale faint golden glow around them marking them as warriors. But something in the way they held themselves, relaxed yet somehow watchful, made her think they might be.

"What do you do for fun in all the little towns where you live?" Delaney asked with a smirk.

Seamus didn't miss a beat. "Chase girls."

"Sorry, but I never run with an open container," Delaney sassed.

The men's rich laughter wafted over them. Involuntarily, Lynnette's eyes drifted back to Riley who she discovered was staring openly at her.

A frisbee flying between them and landing at her feet interrupted their stare down, and she splashed beer on her sandals.

"Alcohol abuse!" Seamus laughed as she shook beer off her foot.

Tilting her head, she shot him a glare from beneath her brows, which only made him laugh harder. Gracefully, she bent her knees, lowering herself enough to retrieve the frisbee without showing off her panties in her short spandex skirt.

"Hey, thanks!" a guy said as he jogged over to their group. "Oh, hey." He gave her a slow once-over. "You want to join us?"

"Um—"

Ugh! Since when was she ever tongue-tied? Uh-huh. She'd lost her voice ten minutes ago when laying eyes on the ridiculously gorgeous man who even now snagged her attention away from the frisbee player. As though she had no control over herself, her eyes strayed to Mr. Hottie—Riley—who stared back at her like he was trying to breach her shield.

As usual, Delaney rescued her. "Sure. Come on, Lynny." Tugging on Lynnette's arm, she led her away, deeper into the party.

"Nice to meet you guys," Lynnette tossed over her shoulder.

Riley saluted her with his beer. "See you in a while."

As the two women walked away, Lynnette whispered into Delaney's ear, "What do you think he means by that?"

"That he thinks you're hot. Which is why we're going to play Bocce frisbee with these other guys for a bit."

Lynnette shot her friend a quizzical look.

"It's good for the super-hot ones to have to work for it."

Seated on a log facing the bonfire, Lynnette entertained herself with watching Delaney torture the local civilian boys with her frisbee-tossing prowess. Having washed out of the game early, pretty much on purpose, she sipped at the dregs of her cup of nasty, watery keg beer and laughed as her friend landed yet another perfect shot over one of the guys' discs. A warm, citrusy smell washed over her, her only warning before Mr. Hottie—Riley—sat down next to her.

"Hello, again."

"Hi."

"Thought you wanted to play." He nodded in the direction of the game where Delaney was currently creaming the civilian guys, most of whom she and her friend knew from town.

"I played—and lost rather spectacularly." At the look on his face, her smile faltered. "Something wrong?"

In a blink, he recovered himself and turned the tables on her with the devastating smile he returned. "Not one damn thing." He shifted closer to her, his heat warming her far more effectively than the bonfire. "Tell me about your beautiful self."

She smirked. "Is that your best pickup line?"

With a shrug, he peeked at her from beneath his brows. "I don't know. Is it working?"

Laughter rang out of her. "What do you want to know?"

"What's your favorite color?"

This close, she could see his eyes were a steel blue.

"Blue."

"Yeah? My favorite is green." He leaned a little closer to her, staring into her eyes. "Yep. Mossy green."

"You don't know your favorite color?" The corner of her mouth ticked up. "Are you always this big a flirt?"

He shifted closer, his jeans-clad thigh sending tingles along the exposed skin below her skirt. For a beat, his eyes dropped to her mouth. The low rumble of his voice vibrated through her. "Is it working?"

Willing herself not to close the distance between their lips, she clamped her knees together and directed her gaze to her hands wrapped around her now-empty cup. "I haven't decided." Sliding him a side-eye, she added, "Maybe," stretching the word almost to its breaking point.

A laugh huffed out of him. "Now who's flirting?"

It was her turn to peek up at him from beneath her brows. She let a smile slip out and blinked when his breath caught.

"We hardly ever cross the mountain to come over here to the Swann. Seems like we've been missing out. I take it you live here?" he asked.

"In the summer."

His brow went up.

"I have a year left at MSU, so I'm only home for the summer." The intensity of his eyes as he stared into her own made her think he was trying to see into her head, but she'd nursed one beer for the last hour and knew her telepathic shield was secure. "What about you? Are you in school?"

He relaxed. "Yeah, I'm a traitor too." Having grown up in the shadow of the University of Montana, they both knew what he referred to—choosing the hated Bobcats over the vaunted Grizzlies. "I wonder how we've never run into each other on campus."

A shrug. "It's a big campus."

"Uh-huh. But you stand out in a crowd."

With a self-deprecating chuckle, she lightly bumped his shoulder with hers. "You truly are a flirt."

A slow heat started on the skin of her left hip. Pleasure radiated out from the spot, settling between her legs. Her eyes flew to Riley's where the firelight revealed an intense curiosity moving across his features. She glanced over her left shoulder, trying to see what was creating a pattern on her skin, a pattern, she was mortified to admit even to herself, that was making her increasingly horny.

"What is it?" he whispered.

It was then she noticed his arm was behind her. "Do you—? Are you—?" Gah! She never had trouble articulating her thoughts. Squirming at the sensations going through her, she said, "Have you been touching me?"

"Depends. What do you mean 'touching' you?" He glanced down at where his thigh was now plastered along hers.

His eyes tracked her tongue as it slipped out to wet her bottom lip and her heart pounded in her chest at the heat she saw in those exquisite blues. The pleasurable sensation began again on her hip, and she arched her back, trying again to see what was causing it.

"What does it feel like, Lynnette?"

"What does what feel like?" On a regular day, she'd never answer in such a breathy tone, but now her core was pulsing in a rhythm with her heart, and she was having trouble concentrating.

"My sign on you."

Her eyes flew to his.

"L-like flower petals." She swallowed. "Like a simple Celtic cross." The sensations intensified even though his touch was butterfly soft. "How"—she stopped to gather her thoughts—"how is this possible so soon?"

He tucked his chin. "What do you mean, so soon?"

"I only turned twenty-one in April."

The corner of his mouth turned up. "Me too. My twin and I completed the sign ritual on the summer solstice."

"See? This is so fast. I don't know of anyone in the community who ever found their mates this soon."

Riley cupped her cheek. "Lucky us, then, to be here together and be attracted to each other from the minute we met."

Lynnette narrowed her eyes. "You think I was attracted to you when your friend Seamus was the one being so charming?"

Instead of taking the bait, he took the cup from her hands and set it on the ground in front of the log. Then he laced his fingers through hers and watched as his calloused thumb traced the pattern over her palm, the same one he continued to trace over her hip with his other hand. "You couldn't tear your eyes from me." He winked. "Which was fine by me because I didn't want to stop looking at you either."

Her thighs quivered as she attempted to fuse them together to keep from embarrassing herself by jumping on his lap and wrapping her legs around his waist. The twin sensations of him tracing his sign over two places on her body put her on the edge of climax, and they were barely touching. Clamping her free hand over his wrist, she held him as she tried to disentangle their fingers. "You have to stop." He blinked at her. "Please." The last word was barely audible to her own ears, but he paused in the middle of tracing his sign.

"What is it?"

Blessedly, her hair curtained her face when she dropped her chin, hiding her embarrassment for the moment. "We're in public."

"No one's watching us."

"They will be if I straddle your lap right here in front of the bonfire."

He wrapped both of his arms around her, pulling her into his chest. Against her temple he murmured, "If it's any consolation, when I stand up, I'm going to offer quite a profile." Air gusted over her cheek as he chuckled at their predicament.

A thought struck her, and she sagged against him. "I still live at home with my parents during the summer."

His body tensed. "Me too." Then he relaxed. "But I know a place we can go. It's up in the mountains between here and Big Fork. It's private and no one will bother us there."

"Now?"

"Of course now." The exasperation in his tone was only marginally less than the look of exasperation on his face.

"But what will we tell our friends?"

"The truth."

CHAPTER THREE

"OME AGAIN?" DELANEY said when Lynnette called her friend away from her game to tell her the big news. "How can you be sure?"

Beside her, Riley lit up. "Because she responded to my sign."

Ever the skeptic, Delaney asked, "How do you know it wasn't overactive hormones from drinking and playing at the party?"

"Did you feel anything?" In the firelight, Riley's eyes twinkled.

"What do you mean, did I feel anything?" Delaney planted her hand on her hip and glared at him. "If you're trying your sign on my friend, how would I feel anything? Unless you meant did she open her shield to me and let me in on what she was thinking? Because the answer to that is no." She shot an accusatory glance in Lynnette's direction.

"I meant, when I tried my sign on you when you were talking to the guy with the frisbee before you stole Lynnette away to play," he said.

Both women gaped at him, but Delaney recovered first. "You tried your sign on me? Why?"

"Because when you turned to talk to your friend, the light from the bonfire was right, and I could see the light rose gold of Scathach's aura around you." Riley shrugged. "Seamus and Rio noticed too. Before you walked out of our little circle, we all tried our signs on you. And you didn't react to any of us."

As though he anticipated Lynnette's words, he tightened his arm around her. "Why didn't you try yours on me then?"

"Delaney and your friend were between us, but Rio tried his on you."

Was that a note of disgust in his tone?

Her brows shot to her hairline. "He did?" Across the picnic area, she watched as Rio and Seamus laughed over something one of the civilians standing near the bonfire said.

Even in the firelight, she noticed a ruddy tinge to Riley's cheeks. "When we saw you sitting by yourself on that log, Seamus and I flipped for who got to come over and talk to you first."

Beside her, Delaney snorted. "Our entire lives hang on the reaction of a talisman responding to a warrior's sign, and you're flipping coins for who gets to give his sign a go." She shook her head in disgust. "Guys are so ridiculous."

Lynnette's laughter rang out. "They kinda are."

Riley shifted from foot to foot, but he didn't relinquish his hold on her. "You didn't think so a few minutes ago."

Pleasurable heat on her hip reminded her even more than his words. She attempted to slow him down by stepping out of the circle of his arm, but he wasn't having it. "Riley," she hissed from the side of her mouth.

"What?" His expression might have been innocent if not for the unholy mischief dancing in his eyes.

Delaney glanced around the assembled party. "I guess I'll be needing to find a ride home tonight." Her glum tone pricked Lynnette's conscience.

"Do you have a car?" she asked Riley.

"Yeah. We brought my Jeep." He smirked and with his thumb

gestured to his brother and friend. "Guess those two will have to visualize themselves home."

"You have my keys, Delaney. Remember?"

Her friend brightened. "That's right." She patted the pocket of her jeans. "You sure you don't need it?"

"Doubt a car can make it up the two-track where we're going tonight," Riley said.

"It's safe, right?" Delaney's concern abruptly changed the mood.

From the time they were little girls, Delaney's inherent need to protect those she cared about surfaced whenever she sensed danger—or thought she did. It came as no surprise when they were teens to discover her friend was a warrior-talisman hybrid. But with her own warrior by her side, Lynnette believed she was safer than she'd ever been, even with her friend's sword arm always nearby.

"Don't worry. Of all the people in the world who want to keep this one safe"—he hauled Lynnette closer to his side—"I'm the first one on the list."

"Hey, this is a party. What has you three whispering like you're planning a crime?" Seamus asked as he and Rio strolled up to them.

"Not a crime," Riley smirked. "More like a getaway."

Rio stared at where Riley's arm wrapped around Lynnette, pulling her flush along his side. "Are you serious? You two are—" He waved a hand between them. "But it's only been two months since the ritual."

The shit-eating grin on Riley's face hinted at some sort of sibling rivalry. Guess she had that to put up with in her future? Growing up an only child, she had no idea how to deal with the dynamic between siblings, especially brothers, especially twins.

"Why are you so surprised, 'big brother'? The girls have always liked me better." Riley wrapped both arms around her, but she had the distinct impression it was more about putting on a show for his brother than being closer to her.

Still, she couldn't help the tiny gasp that escaped her when her front collided with his. Like flipping a switch, he dropped his playful demeanor, his eyes deadly serious as he stared at her parted lips.

"In private, Riley," Seamus said quietly from somewhere behind her, and her warrior seemed to shake himself out of the trance that fell over him when their fully dressed bodies came together so intimately.

"Where are you going?" Rio asked.

"The cabin."

"You sure that's safe?"

Something in Rio's tone lodged trepidation in her chest, but Riley dispelled it with a wink. "We'll be gone a couple days. Tell Mom and Dad not to wait up."

Reluctantly, Lynnette peeled herself away from her warrior's embrace. "Delaney, when you drop off my car, could you let my parents know what's going on?"

Her friend nodded.

"We'll throw a party at the training room when you get home." For the first time since they shared their news, Lynnette glimpsed a real smile on Rio's face. When the guy let his guard down, he was as devastatingly handsome as the man the gods decreed was her fated mate. Too bad Delaney didn't belong to him. They would have made a stunning pair.

"You and Riley are a stunning pair," Delaney communicated telepathically, and Lynnette beamed at her.

"Hey, hey, ladies. None of that here," Rio said. "We don't need to let the nasty ladies know they've lost a Sheridan right out of the gate. Morgan trolls for our family enough as it is."

Rio's comment splashed gallons of ice water over her happiness at being discovered by her warrior so soon after their pivotal birthdays. Because she still touched him, she detected the shiver that stole over Riley too at his brother's words.

"What does he mean?" she asked.

"I'll explain later after we have some things sorted out." Returning his attention to the others he added, "Which we need to do now. See you guys in a few days."

Snagging her by the hand, Riley led Lynnette toward a bright red Jeep ironically parked beside her tiny compact in the parking area.

"You like drawing attention to yourself, I take it," she said as he slipped in front of her and opened her door.

"With my impeccable manners? I'll take that as a compliment." He chuckled.

For a second, she stared at the distance between the ground and the floorboard of the Jeep, wondering how she was going to avoid exposing herself to climb up into it in her short skirt.

"I got you." Riley slipped one arm behind her back, the other beneath her thighs, and lifted her onto the seat as though she weighed nothing. Grinning at her squeak of surprise, he snagged the door, closed it, and jogged around the front of his ride. In one smooth movement, he opened the driver's door and vaulted up onto the seat, pulling the door closed behind him. After digging the keys from the front pocket of his jeans, he fired up the engine. "Buckle up, Buttercup. Wouldn't want you to get bucked out of my Jeep on the road to the cabin."

"Where are we going, again?" she asked as she buckled herself in.

"The Forest Service owns a cabin in the mountains about halfway between here and Flathead Lake. They let hunters and hikers use it as long as they restock the woodpile and leave the cabin in good shape. It's pretty rustic, but it's also *private*."

His emphasis on that word sent shivers over her. Delicious shivers, if she was being honest. So far, they'd only touched each other with their hands, but her training led her to believe that the intensity of the sensations Riley's touch aroused in her was only the opening act to the real event that would be bonding with him.

While he didn't spray gravel when he accelerated out of the parking area, he left no doubt he couldn't wait for the bonding ritual either. The gravel road meant even in his Jeep, he couldn't exceed the speed limit by much, but she noticed he pushed it as far as he could. When they arrived at the T in the road where it met the highway, he set his blinker for a left-hand turn then changed his mind and hung a right into town.

"I thought you said this hunting cabin was between here and Flathead."

"It is, but we might want to eat at some point while we're up there. Is there anywhere open to pick up supplies?"

"No, but I know the code for the convenience store."

He shot her a look.

She shot him one back. "I work there."

A few minutes later, they were loading up a basket with food by the dim light streaming into the store from the office. A couple of packages of sausage, a few dozen eggs, buns, cheese, some packages of hamburger, a pallet of bottled water, and various snacks ended up on the counter when they were finished. Lynnette switched on the computer and checked them out using Riley's credit card. Then she left a note for her boss, so she wouldn't freak out at the after-hours transaction when she discovered it in the morning receipts. They loaded everything into the back of the Jeep. Lynnette carefully reset the alarms for the store and locked up.

Back on the road, she shifted in her seat, tugging at the hem of her short skirt. Riley slipped her a side-eye, and she folded her hands in her lap. With a little distance from the giddy excitement engendered by the success of his sign on her, she couldn't help the awkwardness sliding through her. This was it. Before the night was over, she was going to bond with a man who hadn't existed to her before she saw him sipping a beer near the keg at a run-of-the-mill Lammas Eve bonfire.

For the past sixteen years, her parents had trained her, prepared her for this event, hoping her warrior would discover her before the Morrigan had a chance to steal his life. Yet now that the time was upon her, she worried she wasn't ready. She worried about the two of them discovering her particular skill, the one that perfectly complemented his when they were inevitably called into battle against the war goddesses and their rogue armies. She worried about the bonding ritual and how she was going to react to a man's intimate touch for the first time.

Riley set his hand palm up on her thigh, an invitation. She set her hand on his, and he threaded his fingers through hers, giving her a tiny squeeze. "You said you're in school at MSU. What's your major?"

A weak smile tipped up the corner of her mouth. They'd only known each other a couple of hours, yet already he'd figured out when she needed reassurance—and offered it without fanfare. "I'm a business major. You?"

"Computer programming."

She stared at his calloused hand in hers. "A desk job? Seriously?" After clearing her throat at what she implied, she quickly amended, "It's just that you're so fit, and your hands say you use them harder than typing in code on a keyboard."

"My dad runs a home security business. One day, I hope to open my own branch of it. I spend the summers running cable and power tools when we set up security systems for people." He gave her hand another squeeze. "And I train regularly with other warriors for the battles Morgan insists on waging against us at every opportunity." He paused for a second. "By fit you mean hot, right?"

Hearing the smirk in his voice, she turned her head on the headrest and attempted to dress him down with a look alone. Which was ridiculous in the darkness of the Jeep. "Please tell me you're putting me on and you're not truly so vain."

"What?" He pouted. "You don't think I'm hot?" With another squeeze of her hand, he insisted, "I'm your warrior, your fated mate. You have an obligation to think I'm hot."

His teasing tone drew a reluctant grin from her. Overexaggerating the gesture, she fanned herself. "Oh, yeah. Sooo hot. You should probably roll down the windows before you self-combust."

Riley barked out a laugh. "Seems about right. After all the sweet attention I gave to civilian girls once I discovered how much I like women, I end up mated to a ballbuster."

"*Excuse* me?" Lynnette tugged at her hand, but Riley wouldn't let her go.

"One who needs to learn how to take teasing." His mirth filled the interior of his ride, and after a minute or two, and in spite of herself, she joined him.

Clearing her throat, she asked the important question she didn't know if she wanted answered. "Exactly how much 'sweet attention' did you give civilian girls?"

Riley slowed the Jeep down and made a right turn onto a dirt road. Right away, the ruts and potholes commanded his attention, and he dropped her hand so he could steady the wheel. As he navigated the rough, narrow road, he maintained his concentration on driving with dim light where the forest seemed to swallow the headlights a short distance ahead of them.

Right as she thought he would never answer her question, he said, "My favorite hobby in high school was chasing girls. At some point, I have no doubt my entire family will tell you that, so I might as well be the first one," he said in a self-deprecating tone. If he had any remorse, she didn't hear it in his voice. "My brothers never let me up. Being ten minutes younger than Rio makes me the 'baby' of the family, so the teasing never stops. In middle school when I discovered girls, my shield wasn't very strong yet. And things got way out of hand."

He slowed the Jeep nearly to a crawl as he guided it through a particularly deep and uneven set of ruts. She saw he'd been right about needing a four-wheel-drive vehicle to take them to the private place he knew.

"Dad took pity on me, finally, and drilled me on constructing an impenetrable shield, which pissed off my brothers who lost out on some of their fun hearing what I thought of this or that girl. In high school, I think I had a date nearly every weekend. That pissed off Rowan and Rio too." He chuckled. "The girls in our school all liked me best."

"Considering that the warrior community—not to mention, the gods—expect us to be monogamous, I'm not sure why you're telling me this."

His mood turned serious. "Because I'm trying to preempt all the bullshit you're likely to hear about me. I was a flirt, and I've always been a fan of women. I had a civilian lover, a girlfriend the first year and a half I was in college. I broke it off with her after this past Christmas when it became obvious she thought we were more than we could be." Once again, he slowed the Jeep to crawl over a slab of rock poking out of the dirt on the road. "Every warrior with a brain knows his job after he experiences the sign ritual. I know what's expected of me, Lynnette," he said quietly.

"But you wish you could still play with all the girls." She hated how waspish she sounded, but since she had always kept herself aloof from the civilian boys who chased her, it didn't bode well that she was mated to a self-confirmed flirt.

They bumped over a rise in the road that had her bracing herself with both hands on the dashboard. Ahead of them, the lights flashed on flat space with the dim outline of a building nestled in the trees behind it. Riley pulled up to the front door of what looked like a well-maintained log building and cut the engine. For a long minute, he stared out the windshield then turned to face her. Moonlight limned his features, and he wasn't smiling.

"Yes, I like to flirt, but I've only had one civilian lover. The second you responded to my sign, we started the rest of our lives together." He slid his hand across the back of her seat, his fingers slipping beneath her hair to find the skin on her neck. "I think it's best for that experience to be open and honest. You asked me a question. I answered it honestly." His eyes glittered in the moonlight, and the intensity she saw in them made her shiver. "Before tonight is over, we're going to know each other intimately—very intimately. By morning, there won't be room for anyone else inside either one of us."

She blew out a breath and pulled her lips between her teeth. In the interest of the honesty he'd shown her, she had no choice but to reciprocate. "I've only dated a couple of civilian guys. Nothing serious." Clearing her throat, she added, "Nothing intimate."

He let out a low whistle. "You're telling me you're untouched?"

Balling her hands in her lap, she nodded. "Delaney said when we went to college that I should seek out a nice civilian guy and take care of that. But she always liked boys, so I thought that was more about her than me. Now—"

"Now?" he prompted.

"Now I think maybe some prior experience would have been a good thing."

Reaching across the console, he cupped her cheek in his calloused hand. "I disagree, my beautiful lady. No doubt tonight is going to test my patience at first, but I'm pretty damn happy neither of us has much experience."

Her brows shot to her hairline. "You are? Why?"

"Because it means our bonding is going to be even more secure than that of warrior pairs who've had to wait to find each other. Our race by nature is rather lusty"—he shot her a wolfish grin—"so it's not uncommon for warriors and talismans to take civilian lovers."

"Like you did."

"One," he reminded her. "From your training, you know some take several lovers depending on how many years pass between the sign ritual and finding their mates. But that's not true of us. When we bond, our history will only be us."

CHAPTER FOUR

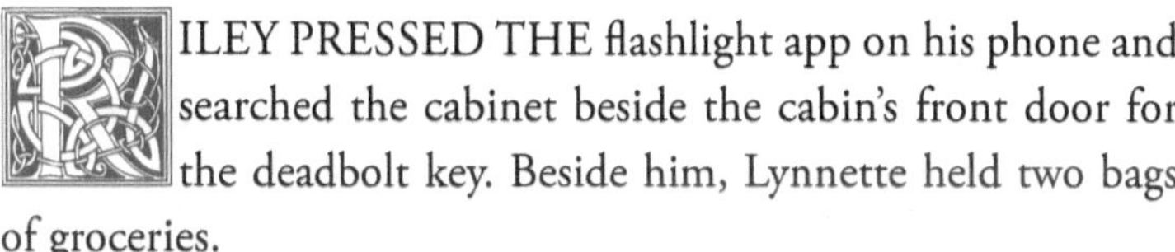

ILEY PRESSED THE flashlight app on his phone and searched the cabinet beside the cabin's front door for the deadbolt key. Beside him, Lynnette held two bags of groceries.

"Finally," he sighed as he produced the key, unlocked the door, and opened it, ushering her inside.

She took two steps into the dark and waited for him. Behind her, he grabbed the other bags of groceries he'd set on the deck and followed her inside. Crossing his fingers, he hoped the lights still worked and patted around on the wall for the switch.

"Wow. I didn't expect this," Lynnette said as the dim overhead light revealed the cabin's interior.

The cabin looked exactly as it had when he'd used it during a hunting trip the previous fall. A neat stack of wood waited beside the woodstove directly opposite the door. To their right was a set of bunk beds and a double bed flanking the window that in daylight looked out into the forest. To the left was a plain pinewood table with four pine chairs beneath another window. Along the wall was an old but serviceable fridge, a short counter with a cupboard above it, and a sink with a hand pump that drew freezing water directly from a well below the cabin.

"Not bad for a rustic mountain cabin, yeah?" He set his groceries on the table.

Her wan grimace said she didn't entirely agree.

"Um, Riley? There's no bathroom."

"Follow me." Taking her hand, he led her back outside and around the side of the cabin where a porta-potty rested on heavy wooden blocks. "Hopefully, it's stocked. If not, I have a roll of TP in the Jeep."

Pulling her hand from his, she wrapped her arms around herself. "Are there bears up here?"

"They're known to frequent this area, yes."

"Is there somewhere else we can go for this bonding ritual? Somewhere I won't have to worry about walking into a bear in the middle of the night if nature calls?"

Pulling her into his arms, he said, "Hey. No bear is going to get you. Not when I'm here with you." He smoothed her hair behind her ear, leaned close, and whispered, "You're with your warrior now. It's my job to keep you safe."

She answered with a full-body shiver, and he hoped it was from his proximity and not her fear of running into a bear in the middle of the night.

"It's not exactly romantic to have your warrior standing outside the bathroom door when you're inside taking care of business."

He couldn't stop the bark of laughter that escaped him. "No judgment, babe."

With a little squeeze, he let her go. "Come on. We have a few more things to unload from the Jeep before we can lock the door against the things that go bump in the night."

"Ha. Ha. You're hilarious."

Peeking at her from beneath his brows, he said, "I know, right?"

With a tiny snort, she stepped around him and headed for the Jeep. He handed her the bedroll he always carried with him while he shrugged into his backpack that held his emergency gear—flashlight, batteries, .45 revolver and spare ammo, first aid kit, bear spray. Even kickass warriors like himself knew they might need something with a little more range than a claymore if they ran into a bear in the woods—or on the way to the privy. When she questioned the weight of the pack as he shouldered it, he winked and grabbed the pallet of bottled water.

"You want to close the door, please?"

She shut the back door to his Jeep and led the way into the cabin.

After she dumped the bedroll on the double bed, she stepped over to where he was putting groceries in the fridge. "Why did you grab that block of dry ice back at the store?"

"The cabin has enough electricity to run the lights. But since it's hit or miss when someone's going to use it, it's not cost effective to run the fridge." By rote, he set the most perishable food on the shelf directly above the dry ice. "Putting a block of dry ice in the bottom usually keeps whatever you store in it cold enough for as long as you're here. And you don't leave a wet mess behind when you leave."

"So this fridge is more of a permanent cooler than a real fridge."

"Pretty much."

She leaned against the edge of the table as she watched him methodically fill the fridge. "How did you know to do all this? I mean, you're pretty well prepared for an impromptu camping trip to the mountains."

He loaded the last of their food into the fridge, closed the door, and leaned against it. "I like to be outside. Hunting, fishing, camping—I enjoy all of it." Crossing his arms over his chest, he added, "Sometimes I need to get away from my brothers."

At her wide-eyed expression he hurried on. "Most of the time, they're great, and we're super close. But the two of them have more of the mythical twin bond than Rio and I have even though we were wombmates."

Her question came out on a strangled laugh. "Wombmates? Is that what you said?"

"We are twins, even though he outweighs me by twenty pounds." Unable to help himself, he puffed out his chest and stood straight. "But I've got him by an inch and a half in height."

"Apparently, you're not competitive with him at all." Even in the dim light, he could see her green eyes twinkling.

"Not one damn bit." He waggled his brows. "When we're training, I win more than I lose when I spar with our older brother Rowan." Drawing in a breath, he finished the thought. "But I don't think anyone can best Rio. My twin is a beast with a claymore."

How that had happened when the two of them formed together would be a mystery he'd never solve. But his way with people made up for what he couldn't approximate with his twin on a battlefield. For the most part, he could talk his way out of anything.

Until he saw the concern in his talisman's eyes.

He cupped her cheek. "Hey. You're not disappointed that Rio's not your mate, are you?"

Turning her head slightly, she nestled her cheek deeper into his palm. "No. He seems to have a hard time smiling. But you don't." The corner of her mouth curved up as she covered his hand with hers, holding him to her. "It sounded for a second there that you were disappointed in not sharing your brother's skills."

Stepping into her, he slipped his other arm around her waist and pulled her body flush with his. "I admit there are moments when I wish Scathach was as excited about me as she is about Rio." He smirked. "Then I watch how hard she works him whenever she shows up at my parents' training room, and I'm a little happy to fly under the warrior goddess's radar."

The silk of her hair drew his attention, and he slid his hand into the warm soft strands at her nape. "So you're an only child. How did you train without siblings?"

"My family is close with the Ferrells."

At the mention of that particular family name, he couldn't help it—he tensed.

"What is it?" she asked.

"Not Tory Ferrell, though. Right?"

Her brow furrowed as she stared into his eyes. "Of course not. Delaney's dad rubbed her uncle's name out of the family tree on the floor of their training room when Tory voluntarily turned rogue. No one ever even mentions him." Tentatively, she set her palm on his chest. The heat from her hand warmed him from the inside out, and he relaxed. "Anyway, I train often with Delaney and her brother Teague. Who, for the record, is a giant pain in the ass."

Her narrowed-eyed expression told its own story. Riley could commiserate with her. "Yeah? So you get what it's like having a big brother even though you don't have one."

"Pretty much."

"Before we leave this cabin, hopefully, we're going to have figured out your skill. But ever since my sign worked on you"—he stopped and blew out a self-deprecating laugh—"even before my sign worked on you, I wanted to kiss you." Pushing his fingers deeper into her hair, he cupped the back of her head and held her. "Do you have any idea how stunning you are?" That last part came out on a whisper, and he heard her quick intake of air. The gods had indeed smiled on him in mating him with Lynnette Montgomery, the most beautiful woman he'd ever encountered.

Taking her response as an invitation, he lowered his head and lightly brushed his lips over hers. And groaned. Petal soft and plush, her gorgeous mouth yielded to his touch, and he increased the pressure. Her arms wrapped around his neck, and she flattened her pillowy breasts against the hard planes of his chest, sending shock waves through his solar plexus. Tightening his arms around her, he sucked a breath in through his nose and dove in. His tongue tasted the seam of her lips for a second before she opened for him. Her wet heat was a heady aphrodisiac tasting of the spearmint gum she'd sneaked earlier and something dark and feminine that had him grinding his center into hers as their tongues tangled together. The tiny moans vibrating in her throat plunged him deeper into the mystery of her perfect mouth as he sealed his lips to hers to explore every delicious part of it. At last, she tore away from his kiss, her breath sawing in and out of her chest as she stared deep into his eyes. He thought his own reflected the wonder he saw in hers.

"That was nothing like the fumbling, pathetic kisses of civilian boys. No wonder my parents were so adamant I never kiss a warrior who wasn't my mate," she said, panting in air. "I could do this with you all night." She tangled her fingers in his hair, her eyes sparkling up at him.

He couldn't contain his happiness. "That's the plan, babe. That's the whole plan."

Reluctantly, he let her go.

"What are you doing?"

"Setting up for all night," he said with a smirk as he headed over to the bed to roll his camping mat over the worn-down mattress. He laid the double sleeping bag over the mat and fluffed the pillow that had been rolled up tight in the middle. At the look on her face, he said, "It's clean. I promise. I ran it through the wash after my last camping trip."

"Okay." The way she dragged out the word and her arms crossed over her luscious rack told him the state of his sleeping bag wasn't what was on her mind.

In two steps, he closed the distance between them. Running his palms up and down her arms, he sought to calm her. Staring deep into her troubled, moss-colored eyes, he willed his libido to hit pause. "Lynnette, you know what has to happen tonight. From the time we're five years old, we all train for our roles in the community. You're a talisman. I'm a warrior. Danu and the Dagda determined the two of us would end up together. In order for our bond to be strong enough to withstand the trials we know we're going to face, we have to complete the bonding ritual." He slid his hands to hers, pried them from their hold around her middle, and twined their fingers together. "I know this is your first time. But as hot as that kiss was, I know our union is going to rock both our worlds." Letting go of her hands, he cupped her face in his palms. "Don't be afraid. We'll go slow."

Though his heart thundered in his chest and his dick throbbed with anticipation of what was to come, he leisurely nibbled at Lynnette's full, soft mouth. Teasing her with light brushes of his lips over hers, he enticed her to take the lead. Her hands found their way around his waist, and he wrapped his arms around her. Still, the kiss remained almost chaste until she slid her tongue along the seam of his lips, licking and tasting until he opened for her. When their tongues met, his body hardened, and he took over again.

The backs of her knees hit the edge of the bed, and she let out a tiny squeak. But he held her upright as he plundered the sweetness of her mouth. In the back of his mind, a smile formed as he registered that she was right there with him. Cool air met the skin on his back as she tugged his T-shirt up his torso. Her soft hands smoothing over his skin left a trail of goose bumps in their wake. He pulled away enough to tug his shirt over his head and drop it on the bed. Lust dilated her pupils as she explored his chest and abs with those hands he already craved to have all over him.

"Wow, Riley. Just. Wow," she whispered as she stared at his exposed skin.

Pushing up on her toes, she kissed along his collarbone to the hollow at the base of his throat then headed south. Her pretty mouth set him on fire as she trailed kisses over his pecs and down the center of his chest to the middle of his abs. Involuntarily, the muscles under his skin rippled at her touch, and he sucked in air.

Peeking up at him, her words came shyly. "You like this? Me kissing you like this?"

"You have no idea." His lips curved up. "Will you let me kiss you like this, too?" he asked as he rubbed his fingertips over her skin where the hem of her T-shirt met the waistband of her skirt.

A slight hesitation, then a nod.

"Words, Lynnette. We're a mated pair, but that doesn't mean I don't need your consent."

She crossed her arms and grabbed the hem of her shirt, pulling it off in one practiced movement. Holding it in her hand, she glanced at the dusty floor and back at him. He didn't need to use telepathy to know what crossed her mind.

Holding up a finger, he said, "One sec," and stepped over to grab a chair, setting it beside the bed. With a smile, she draped her shirt over the back of it and surprised the hell out of him by unclasping her bra and laying it over her shirt.

The dim light revealed her perfection. Dusky, silver-dollar-sized nipples drew up tight on her high round breasts. He rubbed his hands down and up the sides of his jeans to keep himself from reaching out and roughly taking what she offered.

"Words, Lynnette," he croaked out over the lust riding him hard.

"Yes, Riley. I want your hands—and your mouth—on me."

Closing his eyes, he willed some self-control. He set his hands on her waist and pulled her gently into him, his mouth finding hers. For a long moment, he kissed her like they had all the time in the world, but she preempted his good intentions when she moaned into his mouth and rubbed those pretty breasts over his chest. Her restless movements told him the fires licking through his veins tortured her too.

His hands and his mouth met at her breasts. With a breathy "Yes," she arched into his touch as he teased one delicious nipple with quick flicks of the tip of his tongue then sucked it deep into his mouth. She plunged her hands into his hair and held him to her chest as he lavished attention on her sensitive skin with his mouth while he plumped and played her other breast with his work-roughened hand, something he'd discovered quickly she liked very much.

He could have spent all night enjoying her gorgeous rack with his hands and his mouth, but her restlessness intensified under his touch. Her little moans and arching back and busy hands and tiny up-and-down movements with her knees ratcheted up his desire until he thought he might burst the fly of his jeans.

Panting in breath like he'd gone ten rounds with his brothers in the training room, he straightened and cupped her face. "There's so much more, Lynnette. Are you ready?"

Visibly, she swallowed and nodded even as she crossed one leg over the other. "I don't know what's next, but whatever it is, I need it." Her words came out in a rough rasp that had him dragging the zipper of her skirt down even as her hands went to work on the fly of his jeans.

A minute later, their clothes were haphazardly strewn over the chair. Only then as they stood naked in front of each other did Riley stop and take a long breath. When he opened his eyes, he discovered Lynnette staring at his hard length.

"You sure that's going to fit?"

Smiling the smile that had won over every woman he'd ever known, he stepped into her and wrapped his arms around her, letting her feel all of him against her belly. Nuzzling her neck, he whispered into her skin, "The gods made us for each other. We're going to fit perfectly together, like two puzzle pieces making one complete picture."

As he held her, he traced his sign over her, and she gave him what he wanted—access to her thoughts. *"I trust you, Riley Sheridan."*

"My perfect talisman. I promise to make our bonding good for you."

Taking his time, he encouraged her to lie back on the sleeping bag. Then he mapped her olive-toned skin with his hands and his kisses, eliciting sighs of pleasure and moans of desire he could listen to for hours. For a second, she tensed when he traced his fingertip over the sweet petals of her nether lips: then she relaxed and let him in. When he couldn't hold on anymore without being inside her, he parted her legs with his knee and positioned himself at her entrance.

With his eyes locked on her pretty green irises, he slowly pushed inside her until he was balls deep. The velvet vise of her pussy, so wet and tight holding him, was heaven on earth. His body shook with the need to move, but he waited while she adjusted to him.

"How are you?"

She ran her hands up his arms, over his shoulders, and down his pecs. Then she found her way to the vee along his hip bones, and his body took over as he pulled partway out of her and surged deep.

"Oh!" she cried.

He stilled.

A smile curved her lips, and she feathered her fingers over his sensitive skin once more. Again, he surged inside her.

"You like it when I touch you like this," she said, her tone playful.

Huffing out a laugh, he said, "Yeah, I like it very much. But you haven't answered the question."

As she arched her back and pressed her perfect breasts up into him, she said, "I'm awesome." Clutching his biceps, she moved her hips. "I had no idea this was waiting for me when my warrior found me."

"I had no idea either, babe."

She moved again. Though she hadn't said a word, her message came through loud and clear. Riley set a rhythm that had both of them gasping in air. Lynnette wrapped her legs around his waist, closed her eyes tight, and sighed as her inner muscles pulsed hard around his shaft. At last, he let go, pounding his body into her, his climax crackling down his spine and through him into her.

When his arms could no longer hold his weight, he collapsed beside her, sweat sliding off his forehead to collect in his hair.

A minute passed like molasses until he heard her say, "So that's why we're told to wait until our mate finds us. It wasn't what I expected at all."

Rolling onto his side, he pushed up on his elbow so he could look down into her eyes. "Out of curiosity, what did you expect?"

"Pain. A lot of fumbling around trying to figure things out."

A smirk tugged at his lips. "I think I promised you I'd take care of you."

She traced the pad of her finger down the center of his chest and set her palm over his heart. "So you did." Blinking up at him, she added, "I don't know what the gods saw in my spirit to give you to me, but whatever it was, I'm glad. You're something special, Riley Sheridan."

CHAPTER FIVE

INGERS OF LIGHT penetrated the pines surrounding the cabin, waking Lynnette with a sunbeam shining directly at her eyes. Throwing her arm over her face, she took stock of herself. If their first night together was anything to go by, her warrior was an insatiable lover. Yet, she didn't feel any different than she did on other mornings. Other than that she was lying next to a furnace. A grin lifted the corner of her lips. Sitting up, she stretched her arms over her head and shivered.

Beside her, Riley mumbled, "Come here. You're letting the cold air in." He tugged her back inside the sleeping bag and snuggled her into his side. "That's better."

"It is warm in here, but, um, I have to pee." She ducked her head farther down his chest as his soft chuckles vibrated beneath her cheek.

"Do you need an escort?"

"Do bears come out during the day, too?"

"Sometimes."

"Then, yes. I need an escort."

With a long-suffering sigh, he said, "All right. But you don't need to bother with putting on your clothes."

She pushed up enough to look into his

face. "What do you mean, I don't need to put on my clothes? The privy is *outside*."

He chuckled. "Yeah, but we're the only ones here, and you're just going to have to strip out of them again the minute we come back inside."

In her best exasperated tone, she dragged out his name. "Riley."

His answer was to drag her hand down his body where she discovered he was ready for another round of bonding.

"Are you serious?" She laughed.

"As a heart attack." At her raised brow, he added, "Have you seen you, Lynnette? With the sun shining down on all this glorious bed hair"—he fingered the black strands sliding over her shoulder—"and the rosy glow on your cheeks"—he cupped her jaw in his palm and lightly rubbed his thumb over her skin—"and that naughty sparkle in your eyes, I'd have to be dead not to want you right now." His hand slid down her body to grasp her hip. "Don't even get me started on this sexy body of yours. I bet I'll still be waking up like this with you in thirty years. Probably still in fifty years."

"Don't get ahead of yourself, Ace. We haven't even known each other for twenty-four hours."

"Doesn't matter. When my sign worked on you last night, our fate was sealed. The fact we're so compatible together means the rest will be easy." His smile, devastating in the fire's glow and the dim light of the cabin last night, was even more overwhelming in daylight.

"Is it a family trait to be this cocky or just yours?" she half teased him.

His smile morphed into a wickedness that held all kinds of naughty possibilities. "Guess you're going to find out."

"After I use the bathroom. Which I really need to do now."

He huffed out an exasperated snort and rolled out of the

sleeping bag, taking his delicious heat with him. When his feet hit the floor, he swore and shoved his feet into his sneakers. Scrambling out behind him, she nearly jumped out of her skin at the frigid temperature of the polished pine floor under the soles of her feet. Hurriedly, she pushed her feet into her trekking sandals without bothering to unbuckle the heel strap. Riley tossed her his T-shirt and headed for the door in nothing but his shoes.

A giggle escaped her as she dragged his shirt over her head. Abruptly, it stopped in her throat as scents of citrus, musk, and clean sweat engulfed her. She breathed deep and tugged the shirt down her torso. Automatically, she pulled her hair from the collar and fluffed it and caught Riley's stare.

"What?"

"You look incredibly hot in my shirt." He yanked open the door. "Come on. Let's take care of business so we can get back to the fun stuff."

"How are you going to take on a bear in your birthday suit?"

Waggling his brows, he said, "Superhuman speed and cunning. I am a warrior after all."

He held the door for her, and she crossed her eyes at him as she stepped out into an even chillier morning than the one inside the cabin. The sunbeams slipping through the trees radiated a hint of warmth, but she could see her breath in the air when she walked through the shadows to the outhouse. The ambient air temperature pushed her to be quick even as her body protested.

Though she hadn't suffered the discomfort she'd been led to believe would mark her initial experience with sex, the multiple times they'd enjoyed it through the night had left her sore in an oddly pleasant way. Still, she wasn't sure she could give Riley what he wanted right away this morning.

When she exited the porta-potty, he was waiting for her.

"Your turn."

With a smirk, he said, "Nah. The woods worked for me."

She sighed.

Laughing, he took her hand and led her back to the cabin. "You're walking a little different this morning. Are you sore?" The concern in his tone didn't quite match the smugness in his expression.

"Yeah. A little."

"Guess I'll feed you breakfast then, let you rest for a minute."

After he donned his jeans—she noticed he went commando—he headed over to the woodstove and checked the flue. From her warm spot back inside the sleeping bag, she watched him build a fire like it was something he did every morning. Once it started crackling merrily away, he pulled a bowl from the cupboard between the fridge and the sink and cracked eggs into it, returning the shells to the carton. After a quick whip using a fork he grabbed from the drawer beneath the counter, he set the bowl aside and pulled a pan from beneath the sink. He wrinkled his nose and wiped a paper towel over it several times and set it on the burner she hadn't noticed at first. The woodstove wasn't only the heat source for the room but also the cooking heat.

Whistling softly, he opened the package of sausage and dumped it all in the pan. With the fork, he broke it up into chunks and let it sizzle while he prepared a second pan. Lynnette couldn't stop staring at the way his tanned skin accentuated the play of his muscles along his back and arms as he worked. Good manners said she should get up and help, but the show was too much fun to watch.

"You enjoying yourself?" he asked, his cockiness on full display.

"Aren't you too busy to sneak peeks into my thoughts?" With a deliberately snotty tone, she tried to hide her embarrassment at being caught ogling him—and thinking her naughty thoughts while she did.

"We're bonding, sweetheart. We're supposed to leave our

shields open to each other." He buttered a couple of pieces of bread and set them in the empty pan to toast. "Besides, it's good to know my talisman finds me attractive. You know, since I think you're a freakin' smoke show." Over his shoulder, he winked at her and went back to making breakfast.

Her cheeks warmed at his compliment, and she willed herself not to duck beneath the covers. Instead, she crawled out of her warm nest, slipped on her boring white bikini panties and put her skirt back on. After strapping her trekking sandals on properly, she joined him in the "kitchen."

"What can I do to help?"

"Pour some water into that coffee pot over there, spoon some grounds into the filter, and set it here." He indicated a spot on the stove with the bowl of eggs he held before he poured them in with the sausage and gave them a stir.

For a few seconds, she stared at the pump in the sink before she saw the catch and unhooked it. She held the open coffee pot beneath the tap with one hand and tried to pump water with the other. Discovering the pump's strong resistance, she set the pot in the basin and went to work pumping water with both hands. Right when she thought her arms might actually combust, water splashed out of the tap. A bloodcurdling scream escaped her as icy mountain water ran down her arms and covered the front of Riley's shirt, plastering the soft cotton to her chest. Laughter burst from him, and she growled.

"This is not funny! How do I stop this?"

Water overflowed the coffee pot and started filling the basin where the pot blocked the drain.

Taking pity on her, Riley pushed the pump handle down hard and relatched the catch. Then he retrieved a tin mug from the cupboard and poured excess water into it. Over the rim, his eyes danced as he drank the water down, some of it escaping to drizzle down his throat and over his impressive chest.

"See? My chest is wet too, and I didn't scream like the water attacked me." He glanced at his shirt clinging to her curves. "Then again, maybe you're a little more wet."

The heat in his eyes as he stared at her chest went a long way toward warming her even as her cold, wet nipples threatened to poke holes through the thin cotton of his shirt. Riley dragged the knuckles of his free hand over her, sending a lightning bolt of desire straight to her core.

"We can set breakfast aside for a few minutes—"

Her loudly gurgling stomach interrupted his thought.

"Or not," he said with a chuckle. He poured more water out of the coffee pot, added coffee grounds, and set it on the stove. Giving the eggs and sausage scramble a stir, he said, "Why don't you set the table? Everything is in that cupboard"—he nodded in the direction of the one he'd been raiding all morning—"and the drawer below it."

Tugging the wet fabric from her skin, Lynnette couldn't decide what she thought of Riley's apparent chivalry. The way he'd looked at her—and what he'd said about her when they were still in bed—made her feel gorgeous and powerful. This warrior wanted her. But right when his responses to her pooled molten lava low in her belly, he walked away. Maybe breakfast could wait.

"Hey, sweetheart, could you hand me a plate for the toast, please?"

He flipped the toast in the pan and didn't even glance over his shoulder at her. With a sigh, she retrieved three tin plates from the cupboard, handed one to him, and set the other two on the table. The tin cup he'd drunk from joined another she pulled from the cupboard along with knives and forks from the drawer. The fridge yielded milk for her coffee, and she finished off her preparations with napkins and sugar from their stash of dry goods he'd set on the counter the night before.

In minutes, he set breakfast on the table, and the savory

smells of sausage and eggs made her forget her body's other hungers. With a smirk, Riley poured the coffee and returned the pot to the stove. Though the stove hadn't been burning long, the interior of the tiny cabin heated up to cozy, and Lynnette almost forgot about the state of her still-wet T-shirt. His eyes reminded her.

"Since you're not going to do anything about it, you can stop looking at me like that," she snapped and reached for the wooden spatula he'd left in the pan of breakfast.

Covering her hand, he said, "It's not that I don't want everything you have on offer—because I want it all. And I want it all day." His eyes heated to a thousand degrees as his fingers traced a pattern over her skin. "But we have other obligations to each other than the brilliant way the gods determined for us to become a strong pair." The smile he gave her stole her breath. . . and the protest forming on her tongue. "I promise, we're going to do as much bonding as possible over the next few days. But we also need to determine your skill." He let her hand go. "Which is probably going to require some breakfast."

When she didn't immediately spoon eggs and sausage onto her plate, he added, "Come on, Sunshine. Eat up."

Puffing out a sigh, she helped herself to a third of the scramble and a piece of toast she liberally slathered with butter. Riley tipped the pan up and slid most of what she'd left in it onto his plate and added two pieces of toast. She slid him a side-eye, and he shrugged. Before she'd finished three bites of breakfast, his plate was clean and he was eyeing what he'd left in the pan.

"Did you even taste that?"

He smacked his lips. "I'm a damn fine breakfast cook if I do say so myself." Leaning in, he added in a conspiratorial whisper, "Just like my mom." His eyes danced. "You want anymore, or can I finish that?" He nodded toward the pan.

With an extravagant palm-up gesture, she said, "By all means, help yourself." Then she surreptitiously tugged her plate a little to her right, away from him.

Chuckling, he said, "Good move. Especially with the dainty way you eat."

"You mean with manners?" She forked a mouthful of eggs and sausage deliciousness and pretended an inordinate interest in her food.

Laughter burst from him. "You're kind of a spitfire, aren't you? I mean, I kinda got that when we were in the sleeping bag last night, but yeah. Gonna bust my balls whenever we aren't in battle?"

Primly, she dabbed at her mouth with her napkin. "Only when they need busting." Then she coughed to cover her laughter at the answering mirth she saw in his eyes.

Without warning, he slid his hand around the nape of her neck beneath her hair and pulled her to him, kissing her hard and fast, till a smile on his lips turned it playful. When he let her go, he snagged a bite of her breakfast from her plate and popped it into his mouth.

At her outraged gasp, he grinned. "Ball-busting requires payment. You might want to keep that in mind."

Her lips thinned over her gritted teeth as she fought to keep herself from rising to his bait. With what she hoped was a devil-may-care shrug, she returned her attention to her breakfast, even though what she truly wanted was to climb into Riley's lap and show him who was the boss of this pair.

CHAPTER SIX

FTER THEY CLEANED up breakfast, much to Riley's chagrin, Lynnette insisted on wearing her own clothes. The way she filled out his T-shirt made his mouth water. He didn't usually inhale his food the way he'd done that morning, but it was either that or drag her onto his lap and eat her. As much he'd wanted to do nothing but explore their possibilities in bed, he knew they had a responsibility to discover her special skill as soon as possible.

If only they had an enchanted cabin—or some privacy at his parents' training room. Then he could take his time, thoroughly bind her to him with his body before they went about discovering how she would help him in battle. As it was, they only had this private cabin in the mountains and at most a few days before some civilian came along and wanted a turn in the place.

He retrieved his claymore and scabbard from the special compartment where he kept them in his Jeep. Whenever he left the safety of the Sheridan compound up the mountainside from the shore of Flathead Lake, he carried his weapon with him. It meant he didn't have to bend time and space to grab it if he found himself under sudden attack. More honestly, he liked knowing he had it with him at all times.

When he walked back inside the cabin, he stopped still and stared at his talisman who sat at the table with her coffee cup halfway to her luscious mouth as she stared out the window at right angles to the door. A hesitation, then she sipped and set the tin cup on the scarred pine tabletop, wrapping her hands around it as her eyes focused on something beyond the cabin's walls. Delicate bones encased in olive-toned skin created her classically sculpted profile. Her black hair reflected the sunlight streaming through the window behind her. Though she appeared dainty and slight, his experience bonding with her through the night told another story of a fit, strong woman with impressive stamina. Her ball-busting sass was a bonus. Laughter danced in his chest as he tossed his claymore on the bed, stepped over to her, and stole her coffee.

Choking slightly after downing a long drink, he said, "So that's how you're so sweet."

"It's self-defense." She took the cup from his hand and sipped.

His brow went up.

"This stuff you call coffee needs a lot of help to be drinkable."

He pulled his chair up right beside her and reached for her coffee again. "Yeah? Like half the pound of sugar we bought?"

She regarded him with a side-eye. He chuckled and sipped more of her syrupy brew. Usually, he preferred his coffee black, even bitter camp coffee like the stuff in the pot staying warm on the stove, but if he kept stealing drinks from hers, creamy sugar with a shot of coffee might grow on him.

"You brought your sword in. How do you propose we train to figure out my skill?"

Slipping his arm across her shoulders, he snuggled in closer and enjoyed the little shiver that stole over her at his touch. "I guess we begin by talking to each other."

"Uh-huh."

He stole another sip of her coffee. Over the rim of her cup, he asked, "What do you dream about regularly?"

Squirming a bit on her chair, she tugged at the hem of her skirt then folded her hands in her lap. "You mean, do I dream about warriors and battle and the nasty ladies?"

"Among other things." He left the innuendo in the air.

"I don't dream about battle or warriors. Before last night, I'd never seen or heard of you before."

The tin cup hit the table with a thump and his hand flew to his chest. "What do you mean you hadn't heard of me. Everyone in the community knows the Sheridans."

"Well, yeah. I've heard of your *family*." An impish grin twinkled over her features. "But I'd never heard of you, Riley Sheridan."

"You're my talisman. You have no business wounding me like this." Though he attempted to inject the requisite sternness into his tone, he couldn't help the smirk that slipped out. With a dramatic sigh, he said, "Well, I guess we can rule out dreamer as your special skill." He traced the pad of his finger over her forehead and down the side of her face, tucking a strand of silky black hair behind her ear. "Have you seen the future? Worked with a druid on divination?"

"I'm a management major in college, remember? I work from facts and data, not prognostication."

"Which means we can rule out prophetess. What about stories?"

"What about them?"

"Do you like to tell them?"

"Depends. If you mean did I tell some whoppers to get out things I got into when I was a kid, then, I guess?"

"I didn't think you were a bard." His eyes followed his finger as he traced over her skin again. "They're really rare. But I thought I'd ask."

She furrowed her brow, and he pushed the frown away with his fingertip.

"I didn't mean any offense. In the short time we've known each other, I've already figured out you're a special lady. Even if you are afraid of bears." A smirk quirked the corner of his mouth.

With an epic eye roll, she twisted on her chair to face him. "They have been known to eat people. Just sayin'." Sighing, she added, "So what do you suggest we do to discover my skill?" She glanced around at the sparse interior of the cabin. "It doesn't look like the last people to use this place left behind any books on Celtic mythology or bardic traditions." When her eyes came to rest on his, the intensity he saw in their moss-green depths both energized and unnerved him. "I'd rather not be in battle when we discover how I complement your skills." Her hand on his thigh riveted his attention there even as his eyes remained on hers.

Almost absently, she traced her fingers over his jeans, leaving fire in their wake. Fire that burned straight to his cock. "Maybe we should go back to bed, open our shields to each other, and see what comes out of that." Swallowing thickly to cover the hoarse tone of his words, he covered her hand where she traced his sign on him. "Is this how it feels when I trace my sign over you?"

"I don't know." A smile danced in her eyes. "How does it feel?" she asked as she increased the pressure.

"Like my blood has turned to lava," he croaked out over the lust in his throat. Tugging her hand up his thigh, he set it on his crotch. "All of it is right here, ready to erupt."

"Oh!" Her naughty grin grew as she rubbed her palm along his length and gave him the barest squeeze.

In one smooth motion, he settled her to straddle his lap and enjoyed the way her skirt rode high up her thighs. Smoothing his hands over her satiny skin, he pushed her skirt up to her waist, exposing her plain white bikini panties. He slipped a finger inside the thin waistband of her underwear and teased her sensitive skin.

"Riley," she warned.

"Shhh. I'm concentrating." He shot her the smile that worked on every civilian girl he'd ever met.

"I don't think we're going to discover my complementary skill this way." Maybe she was trying to sound tough, but her words came out breathless.

The angle was all wrong. Changing tack, he worried the elastic at the top of her thigh and enjoyed the way she squirmed, bringing her body closer to his. Then he breached the barrier, slipping his finger inside the thin cotton hiding his prize from him. A smile split his lips when he discovered the silky slickness of her arousal. For a few pleasurable minutes, he teased her tight clit with the pad of his finger while he slid his other hand down the back of her panties and squeezed the soft globe that fit his palm so perfectly.

"Riley," she warned again even as her fingers dug into his shoulders. "This is the only pair of panties I have here. You better not tear them."

"Then you should probably take them off right now, or I can't be held responsible for what happens to them." But he didn't remove his hands from where they tested her body.

With a tiny huff, she pushed back on his lap, and like someone was demanding he give up his favorite toy, he let her go. She dropped her panties on the chair she'd recently occupied and shot a meaningful glance at the closed fly of his jeans. He didn't need more of a hint. In a blink, he freed himself and slid his jeans down over his hips, his cock springing up to tap his lower belly. The heat in her eyes as she stared at his shaft left him no choice but to grab her hips and pull her back down on his lap.

"Do you think this chair can stand up to shenanigans?" she asked as she rubbed her slickness along his length, her mouth a breath from his.

"Guess we're going to find out," he said against her lips.

He nipped at her plump lower one and promptly suckled the tiny hurt.

Reaching between them, he positioned himself at her entrance and pulled out of the kiss only enough to say, "Sit on me. Please."

When her body sheathed him, she moaned into his mouth and wrapped her arms tight around his neck. For a long pleasurable moment, he enjoyed the pulsing tightness of being inside his lady before his body demanded he move. Short thrusts were enough of a hint, and Lynnette took over the show. Though she'd been a virgin the previous night, his talisman was a quick study. The way she rode him, her sighs of delight in the act, her hands tugging and bunching his T-shirt at his neck, left him wild with need. His chest heaved as he finished what she started and pulled his shirt over his head to land wherever. With a smile, she crossed her arms in front of her and pulled her shirt over her head. Unlike him, she carefully tossed it onto the nearby chair. A second later, her bra joined it.

"That's so much better, isn't it, Sunny?" he asked rhetorically as he palmed and squeezed the full globes of her breasts. "You are more than I ever hoped to have."

When he set his mouth on her ripe nipple, his name escaped her lips on a sigh, and her body tightened even more around him.

"You like me touching you here with my hands and my mouth," he said into her skin.

"I like you touching me everywhere."

"I like you touching me everywhere," he echoed in his mind with a smirk, his telepathic shield completely open to her.

"Riley Sheridan, you're quite possibly the cockiest man I've ever met."

He sucked her hard, and she squeaked and increased her rhythms over him.

"But you back it all up." Even telepathically, her words came out on a sigh.

"Damn straight I do."

When her rhythms couldn't keep up with their excitement, he grasped her hips and took over. Beneath him, the chair groaned and creaked. Above him, Lynnette sighed and moaned. Throwing her head back, she thrust her luscious rack in his face and keened her climax to the ceiling. He fastened his mouth to the side of her breast and pumped harder until ten thousand watts of electricity crackled down his spine and his body seized as his life force shot up into her. Thunder rumbled in his throat when the aftershocks hit and he rocked up into her pulsing body again and again.

A splintering crack was their only warning when the wooden chair gave way. With an "oomph!" Lynnette landed in a heap on top of his chest. His back settled hard into the slats of the chair back when the chair gave way and dumped them on the unforgiving floor.

Beneath her, he groaned. "That's gonna leave a mark."

She sucked in a breath and started giggling. When her giggles morphed into uncontrollable laughter, her body heaving over top of him, he gave in and joined her.

Half the morning later when her laughter finally subsided, she said, "Guess we owe the Forest Service a chair." She hiccuped and pushed up on her knees. "Ouch!" Gingerly, she sat on the floor beside him and inspected her bright red kneecaps. "Looks like that was only a good idea on paper," she added as she rubbed her knees.

"It was a great idea. Next time, we'll use a sturdier chair." He sat up and kissed her owies.

Though she gifted him an epic eye roll, he caught the curve at the side of her expressively sculpted mouth. In one lithe movement, he jumped to his feet and ignored the twinge the slats of the chair left behind on his back. Offering her his hand, he pulled her up and wrapped her in his arms, his mouth absorbing the "Oh!" that escaped hers. Her full breasts flattened against the wall of his chest was another kind of heaven he already craved and knew would be a truth for the rest of his life.

A shadow obliterated the sunlight, instantly plunging the temperature in the cabin twenty degrees, even as the woodstove did its job in the corner. Both of them shivered in the afterglow of their latest round of bonding, but an ominous sense of foreboding stole through him.

"You feel it too."

"I think our pairing has been noticed by some entities who aren't happy about it," he communicated to her.

"Now what?"

"Now I think we have no choice but to try to figure out what your skill is."

Reluctantly, he let her step out of his arms and over to the chair to re-dress herself.

"Do you think it's a good idea to discover my skill without the benefit of at least some druidic enchantments over us?" she asked as she arranged herself in her bra.

Her movements momentarily drew his attention away from the conversation. When she caught him staring, she wrinkled her nose at him and wasted no time tugging her shirt over herself. She barely showed him any skin when her panties disappeared beneath her skirt, which she smoothed down her thighs.

Shaking himself out of his lust-filled thoughts, he zipped his fly and went in search of his T-shirt, discovering it on the floor beside the bed. "Our circumstances aren't ideal, but you met my twin and my friend last night at the bonfire. Do you think we'd have any sort of privacy if I'd taken you home to my parents' place?" He picked up his claymore from where he'd tossed it on the bed and removed it from its scabbard. As he inspected the blade, he said, "Didn't your parents teach you that training without proper bonding might help a warrior-talisman pair discover the talisman's skill, but it won't give them the essential oneness required of a strong fighting unit?"

The look on her face told him he needed to lay out all his cards. He set his weapon back on the bed and stepped over the mess of broken chair in the middle of the floor. Taking her hands in his, he stared into her endlessly fascinating moss-colored eyes. "I'm the first of my brothers to find his mate. They've always flipped me shit about being the youngest, being the ladies' man, being the one they could best in the training Dad and Scathach drill us on regularly."

"Scathach?" she gasped. "You train regularly with the warrior goddess herself?"

With a shrug of his shoulder, he said, "Yeah. She has a soft spot for my family. Has had for about a millennium." A self-deprecating laugh huffed out of him. "If you call working us into a sweat for days a soft spot. Anyway, I'm the first one to find his talisman, and I want us to learn each other without their inter-ference or commentary." He glanced around the interior of the cabin. "This place is secluded. And we have no reason to think it would be on the nasty ladies' radar."

Lynnette sucked air in through her nose and blew out a breath. "Riley. The war goddesses don't key on places. They key on people. You know that." With a little tug, she slipped her hands from his and walked over to the window beside the door. "If Scathach harbors a special interest in you and your family, it wouldn't surprise me to find out the unholy trinity of war keeps tabs on you too."

It occurred to him that by some unspoken agreement, the two of them had decided not to name the goddesses who regu-larly trolled for warriors—especially unbonded ones—either to attack or to entice them into their terrible army of rogues. The thought left him uneasy.

"You're right. As much as I'd rather spend the rest of this

weekend"—he stepped over and rested his chin on her shoulder—"and all of the foreseeable future doing nothing but exploring the possibilities of your luscious body and quick mind, we need to do the necessary work of discovering your skill." He squatted down and picked up the broken legs of the chair they'd damaged. Upon closer inspection, he amended his assessment from damaged to destroyed. Gathering up the remains, he walked them over to the pile of wood in the bin near the stove. "We probably shouldn't train in here, what with the fragile furniture and all," he said, not bothering to hide his smirk. "It's warmed up considerably since our trek to the outhouse earlier." At her dubious expression, he added, "I promise."

CHAPTER SEVEN

LYNNETTE WISHED SHE had half of Riley's optimism that training in the open was a good idea. Yet she had no choice but to trust him. After all, he'd trained "regularly" with Scathach, the supreme warrior trainer herself.

This high on the mountain, the silence echoed around her. Closing her eyes, slowing her breathing, and holding herself still, she focused her hearing on the forest surrounding the cabin and the parking area in front of it. After a minute or two, she discerned the gurgling sounds of water flowing over rocks in a creek somewhere nearby. In the distance, an eagle screamed as it flew over the pines. Tiny rustlings in the undergrowth told a tale of small animals going about their daily business of securing food. Riley's footsteps on the gravel between the side of the cabin and the porta-potty warned her of his return before he came into view around the corner of the building.

"I didn't see or feel anything in the area that should worry us," he said as he joined her. "You ready?"

Steeling herself for the unknown, she pasted on her best smile and nodded. "Ready as I'll ever be."

"Uh-huh." He packed a metric ton of

skepticism into that two-syllable utterance. Then he swooped in and smacked a kiss on her mouth.

Staggering forward a step at his unexpected move, she blinked at him. "What—"

He winked. "Now you're ready." Drawing his sword from the scabbard on his back, he began a series of lunges and stretches. When she remained still, watching him, he said, "You should probably warm up too. No doubt this is going to be strenuous."

Imitating his movements, she stretched her arms and legs. When he high-stepped in place, she did too. By the time he'd stopped moving, her signal to rest too, she'd worked up a sweat she wiped off her forehead with the hem of her shirt while the fabric clung to a light sheen of moisture on her back.

"I'm going to reenact battle scenarios Scathach has used to train us. I'll keep my shield open so you can see what I see in my head. As I move, see if you can anticipate where my enemies are going to come at me from or what I should do next."

Tilting her head to one side, she asked, "Why? In spite of your earlier interrogation, do you think I could be a dreamer?"

"I've no idea what you are, but this is what my parents do when they train, so I thought we'd give it a try."

Accepting his explanation with a nod, she stood to one side of the open parking lot, opened her shield, and concentrated on seeing into his thoughts. As he moved, she saw that he battled a small band of rogues in a tight alleyway in some suburban setting. Idly, she thought training this way was like watching someone play a video game. Riley snorted a laugh, but that was his only response to her fleeting thought as he thrust and parried, danced away from a blow, spun, and thrust again. More rogues joined the three or four involved in the initial attack, but she didn't see them coming until they were there, their claymores seeming to attack her warrior like a swarm of bees.

"You didn't see them coming?" Though he communicated telepathically to her, his labored breathing pounded in her ears.

"I'm sorry. No."

The speed of Riley's blade in the dappled sunlight falling through the trees mesmerized her. Until it stopped. Abruptly. Only then did she figure out he'd tuned into her hearing the distant barking of a dog.

Exchanging a concerned glance with her warrior, Lynnette said, "You said we'd have the cabin for a few days."

"That's what I thought." He leaned his forehead on the hilt of his claymore as he caught his breath. Another bark came from the direction of the creek. "If that belongs to a hiker, the person is probably in trouble. The slope down to the creek from here is wicked steep. Not something you could hike easily. Or at all." Nodding his head in the direction of the road, he added, "The trail veers off from the road about a quarter mile back. It's a cakewalk to the water from there. But as you move farther upstream, the terrain changes abruptly from one step to the next, from easy mode to impossible."

The barking increased in volume, nearly blocking out his next words.

"I don't think any animals, let alone people, can climb the slope immediately behind the cabin."

As he spoke, a snarling, snapping bark came from the corner of the cabin exactly where Riley had said it couldn't. Lynnette's hand flew to her mouth to cover her scream as a creature she thought only existed in Irish myths faced them.

Riley straightened, his weapon aimed at the monster. "What the hell?"

"Is that—" She swallowed and tried again. "Is that what I think it is?" Taking one slow step and another, she positioned herself behind her warrior.

The thing snapped its jaws and snarled and barked again.

Though it seemed to amble, in one breath it moved from one end of the cabin to the other, effectively cutting off their ability to escape to the inside of the building. Not that either of them had any delusions that a beast of this size and ferocity couldn't find its way through a window of the cabin if it wanted inside.

"Looks like Morgan has an idea I've discovered my mate."

Behind him Lynnette gasped. "Is that what that is? A warning?"

"No. A direct threat. *Dobhar-chù* prefer people for dinner. The way that thing is angling its head, I'd say it fancies eating you." He chuckled. "Can't say I blame him. I'd like to eat you too, but you'd enjoy the way I do it."

Through clenched teeth, she said, "How can you be thinking about that at a time like this?"

"Because I can feel your heat on my back, and I caught a whiff of sex when the breeze shifted and your scent blew over me." She didn't need to see his face to know a cocky grin spread over it at the memory of what the two of them had been doing only a little while earlier.

She wanted to smack him, but the half-dog, half-otter, man-eating creature the bards of Ireland called a dobhar-chù barked again, the crack of sound splintering the air around them. Doing her best to keep her voice steady, she said, "According to legend, these creatures don't tend to be loners. Do you think it has friends?"

"Undoubtedly. Morgan will want to split us up, take one or both of us before we're fully bonded. Usually, she attacks with rogues, but I guess those pansies didn't want to make the climb up here." Shifting on the balls of his feet, he readied himself for attack.

"Now what? We've barely started training, and we don't have the faintest clue what my skill is. How am I going to help you against this thing?"

The dobhar-chù barked again, and suddenly, three more of the monsters materialized out of the forest behind it.

Audibly, she swallowed hard. "So they come in packs?"

"What are you saying? There's only the one." Riley shifted his stance, holding his claymore in front of him with both hands on the hilt.

"Can't you see the other three coming up the hill behind it?"

"You have X-ray vision? I can't see past the one in front of us."

She stilled, her hearing trained on another sound. "The dobhar-chù isn't our only problem," she whispered.

"What are you saying?" The hoarse sound of his voice riveted her eyes to the immediate threat in front of them.

"People are coming. Six or eight of them through the trees from above us. They're trying to step quietly, which means they probably aren't civilians—or friendly." All she wanted to do was wrap her arms around Riley and disappear. At that thought, a wave of icy air rippled over her. Though she'd never met a goddess in person before, she had a clue that the sudden change in temperature wasn't a fluke of nature.

"Shit. I thought we could get away with this," he hissed. "I thought we could hide out up here in the middle of nowhere and learn each other, train together, fall for—"

The snarling bark of the one dobhar-chù that had drowned out their earlier conversation was weak sauce compared to when its three friends joined it. The growling, snarling barks echoed through the forest, and she glanced around, fearful the noise would topple nearby trees on them.

That's when she saw the first rogue emerge from the forest.

"Rogues, Riley."

"You need to hide. Visualize yourself somewhere nearby."

Under the guise of hugging him around the waist, which she desperately wanted to do anyway, she sneaked the keys to his Jeep from his front pocket.

"Running over rogues probably isn't sporting, but neither is taking on a lone warrior at six-to-one odds with a pack of man-eating monsters as distractions."

Even in her mind, she could hear him smiling. *"Maybe not, but I like the way you think."*

Lynnette loathed the idea of leaving her warrior alone with the terrible odds they faced, especially with their cluelessness about her skill. But she had no choice. As a talisman, she couldn't fight either the rogues or the monsters in hand-to-hand combat. She only had her wits and a deep, compelling need to save her warrior, one she neither understood nor questioned.

The first thing she noticed from the hiding place she'd visualized herself to in the back of the Jeep was her intensified hearing. A rogue had crossed the road behind the Jeep with a clear idea of flanking Riley. *"There's a rogue in the trees behind you to your right. If you bend time and space backward at a forty-five degree angle for about twenty yards, you should land with the tip of your claymore at the base of his spine."*

It took all her willpower not to poke her head up and check out the window of the vehicle to see if Riley followed her directions. After the way she hadn't seen any of the rogues in the scenario they were practicing before reality showed up, she couldn't blame him for not listening to her. Yet she truly hoped he gave her a chance. And that she was right.

A scream coming from the direction of the rogue rent the air. *"Are you all right?"*

A grunt greeted her ears when she expected a response in her mind. Her heart leaped into her throat as seconds stretched into days.

At last, he said, *"The rogue had a friend."* A pause. *"I landed on him. Surprised the hell out of both of us."*

That made no sense. She'd only heard one set of footsteps sneaking through the undergrowth.

"For some reason, one rogue piggybacked the other."

Wrapping her hand around the frame of the back seat, her knuckles turned white with the effort to keep herself from poking her head up from her hiding place, an idea dawning on her. *"How are you?"*

"Awesome, of course."

God, the man was cocky. How could he be so sure of himself with the odds they faced? As if to punctuate the thought, the pack of dobhar-chù blasted the air with their cacophony of barks, snarls, and growls. The hairs on her body stood at attention as the unholy racket seemed to vibrate the Jeep to life. A whoosh of air buffeted her hiding place as the pack of monsters raced by.

"The cabin door! Jump to the cabin door! You can keep the five rogues coming at you from the trees from surrounding you."

Even with using their telepathy, she couldn't be sure he heard her in the din of the pack of dog-otter monsters racing in the direction of the downed rogues.

"How do you know where they are? Did you see them?"

"Are you in front of the cabin?"

If the situation weren't so dire, she would have laughed at his huffy sigh. *"Of course. Only a stupid warrior ignores the advice of his talisman. Now answer the question."*

"I tracked the sounds of their movements."

"Brilliant, Sunshine! Now we know what your skill is." A pause.

Those pauses were going to drive her straight up the wall. She wished she could see what was going on, but she didn't dare sneak a peek and give away her hiding place.

"What's going on?"

No response.

"Riley? What's happening?" She gripped the frame of the seat harder, determined to keep the desperation squeezing her heart from coming through in her thoughts.

The uneven crunch of feet running across gravel assaulted

her ears, forcing her to concentrate on counting footsteps to figure out how many rogues had broken cover. For a second, she thought she heard sword blades clanging together and shearing off each other. Then the eardrum-crushing discordant racket of the dobhar-chù overwhelmed every other sound in the clearing. Squeezing her eyes shut and gritting her teeth against the onslaught of noise, she worked to hear her warrior's thoughts through the din.

"Damn it, Riley. Tell me what's going on."

Again, the rush of air as the monsters raced past the Jeep toward the cabin rocked her hiding place on its wheels. She gripped the stanchions anchoring the seat with both hands and curled herself into the tiniest ball she could tuck her five-foot-five-inch frame into. A headache pounded into her brain as she tried to concentrate on hearing the important sounds through the noise.

Then all at once: silence.

Infinitesimally, Lynnette relaxed each part of her body, beginning with her closed eyes and clenched jaw. Like waves flowing out from a rock cast into a pond, the silence spread. A cloak of dread settled over her, and she called desperately to her warrior. *"Riley! Riley! Where are you? Please, don't be gone."* A sob escaped her. *"Don't be Morgan's prize when I've only known you for a day."* Though she'd done her best to exude strength and confidence when she directed him as their enemies moved in, she couldn't maintain that strength in the absence of his response.

Double-checking her shield to make sure it remained open to her warrior, she waited in her hiding place for minutes that stretched into infinity. Slowly, she lifted her head enough to see out of the bottom of the windshield where the Jeep faced the cabin. The disturbed gravel in front of the door told a story of pitched battle, but that was all.

"Riley?"

Having no other choice, she took a chance and exited the Jeep. The light snick of the door as she carefully pushed it shut echoed in her ears in the absolute silence of the parking area. *No! He can't be gone. Not when we've only been together a day.* Wrapping her arms around her middle, she gingerly made the short journey to the cabin. Instead of walking through the door, she sneaked up to the front window and scanned the Spartan interior. Nothing looked amiss from how she and Riley had left it when they stepped outside into hell.

Now what?

CHAPTER EIGHT

A SNUFFLING SOUND, LIKE a large animal walking up the road behind her, rocketed Lynnette's heart rate into the stratosphere. She spun on her toes, balancing to run or to visualize herself elsewhere, and came face-to-face with a medium-sized grizzly.

"Shit," she hissed. "You're all I need right now."

"Actually, you do need me."

"*What?*" Lynnette gasped and shook her head. "I must be losing it."

If she didn't know better, she could have sworn the creature bared its teeth in amusement.

Sliding one slow step toward the cabin door, she attempted to escape inside when the bear gave itself one mighty shake. Before her eyes, the beast transformed into a woman a few inches taller than Lynnette with the ripped musculature of someone who competed in body building regularly. Her russet hair flowed down her back in coarse waves. A gossamer sheath the same color as her hair covered her body from her shoulders to midthigh. But it was her ice-blue eyes that riveted Lynnette's attention.

Throwing her shoulders back, Lynnette went for exuding confidence she was far from feeling. "Are you a goddess?"

"I wish." The woman chuckled. "I'm a shaman. Of the shape-shifter variety rather than the prognosticator or rituals sort, as you might have guessed." With a smile, she extended her hand. "Renleigh Rogan. And you are?"

"Lynnette Montgomery." When their hands met, the woman's calluses surprised her.

"I thought I heard the barking of the dobhar-chù, so I decided to investigate." Nodding in the direction of the rogues Riley took out during the fight, she said, "From the bits of men I saw on the edge of the road, someone was sacrificed for their lunch."

"Rogues. They attacked after the dobhar-chù arrived." She slumped back against the side of the cabin, the events of the morning overwhelming her. "They attacked my warrior with at least six-to-one odds plus the monsters." Swallowing over the lump forming in her throat, she added, "He's not answering me. Even telepathically." *I can't lose him. I just can't.*

Renleigh crossed her impressive arms over her chest and gave Lynnette a once-over. "Let me guess. You were training out here in the open."

Lynnette's eyes saucered. "How did you know?"

"I have a little place down the road from here. When I was chanting reinforcements over my outer barriers, I sensed a ripple in the cosmos and knew a warrior was nearby." She glanced around at the disturbed gravel in front of the cabin. "But this didn't happen when your warrior and you were training."

"No. We'd barely started when we heard the unearthly barking of the dobhar-chù. Then I picked up the sound of the rogues making their stealthy way through the trees, and the next thing I knew, I was hiding out in the Jeep while Riley took on a small army by himself."

"You were bonding here? Why?"

"Riley—well, both of us—wanted somewhere private."

Renleigh's eyes took on a world-weariness in the massive eyeroll she gifted Lynnette. "Private and *enchanted* would have been a good move."

Lynnette shot her a "duh" look. "I have to find him, help him somehow." Smacking her hand on her head at the obvious answer she hadn't thought of, she said, "Excuse me for a minute." Reaching out telepathically, she hoped Rio, being Riley's twin, would be tuned in to him or at least open to communicating with her.

"I just remembered my warrior's twin lives nearby. I'm reaching out to him." Closing her eyes, she pictured the man she'd met at the bonfire the night before. *"Rio? Riley's in trouble. We need help."*

Nodding her approval, Renleigh silently waited. Oddly, the shaman's presence, even when berating Lynnette for their mistakes, gave her a measure of calm in the middle of the shitstorm she found herself in.

"Rio? Please. It's Lynnette. We've been attacked. Riley's gone, and he's not responding to me via telepathy."

After an age of waiting for Rio to respond, she made up her mind to find a way on her own. Her intuition told her Riley didn't have much time, and she couldn't waste it waiting for his brother to open his shield when she banged against it.

"His family isn't responding to my pleas for help. To be fair, I only talked to his twin for a few minutes at the party where we met before Riley dragged me away to come up here." She bit her lip. "But I would have thought they are close enough that Rio would sense when Riley needs him." When she glanced away to surreptitiously swipe at a tear she couldn't stop, a weird shimmer in the gravel grabbed her attention.

She took a step over to where she saw the blue-green reflection and knelt to check it out. "What the hell?" It was a footprint with the claws of an otter and the pads of a dog. Narrowing her eyes, she followed the direction it pointed and saw another and another and still more. Standing, she surveyed the area where she picked up more and more tracks. "This makes no sense. There were four dobhar-chù, but only two were here in front of the cabin, their attention trained, I would guess, on my warrior."

Following the tracks, she ended up at the back of the cabin. A small clearing there showed more signs of struggle, this time between men. It looked like three or four were struggling with one. *Riley!*

Renleigh came up behind her. "What is it? What has your attention?" The excitement in her voice made her sound younger than she first appeared when she was berating Lynnette about training with her warrior out in the open.

"There." She pointed at the disturbed earth between the cabin and a thick line of pines behind it.

Renleigh squinted at the ground and glanced back at her. "What's so special about the grass?"

Lynnette tucked her chin, her brow furrowing. "You're telling me you can't see all the tracks? The evidence of a fight?"

With a shrug, the shaman said, "Looks like grass and dirt to me."

"Um. The tracks lead back here." Lynnette started walking to the edge of the clearing. Under her breath, she mumbled, "You're a shaman. How can you not see something so obvious?"

Renleigh grabbed her elbow, hauling her up short. "Wait. You can't go where those tracks you say you can see are leading."

Lynnette glared at her. "I am not abandoning my warrior to whatever terrible fate the Morrigan has planned for him."

"I'm not suggesting that." Gently, she edged the two of them to the trees. "But if the rogues and the dobhar-chù took your warrior this way, you can't follow." She indicated the area beyond the tree line and Lynnette saw what the shaman meant.

Tears filled the back of her throat: her shoulders slumped in defeat. The trees clung to a sheer drop-off. Only the magic of a goddess could have prevented the rogues and monsters from sliding to a terrible end at the bottom. Wrapping herself around the narrow circumference of a sturdy trunk, she leaned over as far as she could to confirm her suspicions. The iridescent blue-green tracks that first caught her eye in the gravel in front of the cabin and led her around to the back traveled directly down the super-steep mountainside as though the men and monsters had defied gravity to take a midmorning stroll. Except for one man. The tracks indicated someone being dragged along with the others. Somehow, the rogues subdued her warrior and dragged him away with them.

Turning wild eyes on her new ally, or who she hoped would be her ally, Lynnette said, "I can't follow them this way, but Riley told me this morning the creek gurgling down there"—she gestured down the hill with her thumb—"is easily accessible from a trail down the road a ways. I should be able to intercept these tracks where they reach the creek and pick up Riley's trail from there."

"I know a faster way."

Renleigh lowered her head and closed her eyes. With a mighty exhale and a shrug of her championship swimmer-like shoulders, her body transformed. In a blink, a mighty eagle stood where a woman had been standing a second before.

Involuntarily, Lynnette jumped back. The foot-long talons on the creature were fearsome enough, but the wickedly hooked beak could snap her in half. The bird turned in a half circle and glanced over her shoulder. "Climb on."

⋙

"They're dining on you or us. We prefer it to be you," the rogue clinging to Riley's sword arm said as the three rogues half-dragged, half-fought him as they traveled a rocky path along the stream.

The blow one of them landed to the top of his head still

throbbed, and his fuzzy vision contributed to his inability to anticipate the path in front of him, infuriating him with his stumbling gait. "That's still up for debate."

Mirthlessly, the man laughed.

Somewhere ahead of them, he heard the crashing of large animals in the water. The dobhar-chù preferred water travel whenever it presented itself, but they didn't use otter stealth mode today. Guess they were confident in their meal, or satiated enough from the three dead rogues they'd already devoured, to care. He doubted any of that noise was playful—or meant to be.

Why the Morrigan would use the dobhar-chù on a lone warrior was anyone's guess. But he took comfort in knowing Lynnette remained safe at the cabin. All the rogues who'd attacked them were dead or going to find themselves that way—as soon as his head cleared. No matter what the old witch had planned for him, no way was he pleasuring her with his blood—either in her unholy bed or by crossing the ford into the mists. Not after he'd had so little time with his talisman. In a single night, Lynnette showed him why she was his perfect mate. Her fire and strength, her resourcefulness, her willingness to play with him, the sparkle in her eyes when she called him out for being cocky—his woman was the whole package. Her smoking-hot body, those gorgeous green eyes, and that glorious mass of black hair he already loved to tangle his fingers in were a bonus.

The rugged path smoothed out for a few steps as the trail opened into a clearing. The marshy-looking expanse didn't improve his attitude. Such a place lent itself to aquatic creatures and wouldn't allow for easy maneuvering in battle. A red-black shimmer hovered into view a few feet in front of him. In a blink, the great war goddess herself, the Morrigan, stood in front of him.

"You discovered your talisman rather more quickly than any of us could have anticipated." A trail of prickly heat seared the skin between his pecs where the goddess dragged a blood-red fingernail. "Being a Sheridan, though, you could not contain your cocksure belief that you are equal to the gods." She crossed her arms over her chest, her glowing red eyes taking on an otherworldly intensity. "Training with your talisman out in the open made it disgustingly easy to locate you, plan for you."

He bared his teeth at her but remained silent. Training with Scathach had taught him that when a goddess had all the power, it was best to wait her out.

"You may have noticed that your telepathy with your talisman is nonexistent. You see, I have cloaked this area against your supernatural abilities. Here, you are on your own with the odds in my favor, naturally."

Her laughter, like dry sticks rubbing together, grated on his nerves. Still, he kept his silence. No doubt she saw the defiance in his stare. Being mortal, he had a finite amount of time on the planet, but he determined he wouldn't see the end at a too-short twenty-one years. He wouldn't see the end alone without his talisman near him.

Morgan's patience wore thin. "You have nothing to say, Riley Sheridan?" When she took a menacing step toward him, the rogues holding him shrank away a little. "You defy me with your silence?" The booming of her voice rocked the trees surrounding the clearing.

Riley held his ground.

"We will see how you do when you face four hungry dobhar-chù on their turf." She nodded at the rogues holding him. "Release him."

The third rogue at Riley's back—who had stolen and held on to his claymore—screamed when Riley spun on his heel and tore it from the man's scabbard, opening a gash in the back of the rogue's head. With one quick move, he brought the hilt down on the man's skull, finishing the job. Lightly, he jumped over the body with the notion of retreating back up the path. The uneven ground and surrounding trees would give him better odds against the dobhar-chù than taking them on in the watery swamp as the Morrigan planned. Her rogues might fight battles according to her dictates, but he wasn't one of the war goddess's adherents. Besides, Scathach had taught him better battle tactics than to take on an enemy in the space of the enemy's choosing.

The other two rogues bent time and space to block his escape and force him back to the swamp. Guess they had some tactics too. The piercing scree of an eagle flying overhead penetrated the clashing and clanging of steel on steel, but Riley couldn't look away from the battle in front of him. Then a comforting warmth stole over him and he opened his shield to his patron goddess. When Lynnette's voice echoed in his head instead of Scathach's, he stumbled a step.

"The dobhar-chù are nearby. They'll be easy to kill when their attention is distracted by feasting on those rogues. Let them push you back toward the swamp."

"Where are you?" He slashed at the rogue bearing down hard on him from his left, slicing cleanly through the man's leather armor and leaving a gaping wound in his chest. As though the wound meant nothing, the rogue pressed on.

"Don't worry about me. Concentrate on your job."

Taking his weapon in both hands, he pirouetted on one foot and swung his claymore in a deadly arc, severing the rogue's head from his body. The man's eyes saucered in surprise, his mouth working with no sound before his forward momentum dropped his head on the ground in front of his body. In the close confines of the tree-lined path, Riley had to pull his swing up short to avoid embedding his sword in the bark of a pine as the rogue's body dropped in front of him like a felled tree.

"Damn it, Lynnette. You shouldn't be anywhere near here."

"Morgan—excuse me—the Morrigan enchanted this area against our telepathy. I have to be here. It's the only way I can help you."

The last rogue standing took advantage of Riley's momentary lapse of concentration to open a gash on his upper arm. His hissed breath through clenched teeth was his sole response, but somehow his talisman heard it from wherever she'd hidden herself.

"Pay attention to your job, Sheridan. The dobhar-chù will key in on your blood every bit as much as on the rogues'. You possess supernatural abilities, not immortality."

The exasperation in her tone came through loud in his head. A cheeky smile spread over his features. Obviously, she planned to bust his balls every chance she got. He planned to give her a lifetime of chances.

"What's so funny, Riley Sheridan?" the last rogue standing gritted out.

"My talisman."

"Liar!" With a scream, the rogue repositioned his weapon in his hands and came at Riley like a buzz saw. "She can't reach you. Morgan saw to that."

Learning that tidbit pissed Riley off like nothing else. The rogues knew what Morgan had done? No wonder they'd been so cocky before.

He shouted for the goddess's hearing wherever she'd gone to watch the show—he had no doubt she was somewhere nearby delighting in the carnage regardless of whose blood was spilled. "Will the dobhar-chù spare enough blood for your desires, Morgan? Or will they lap it all up and leave nothing for your pleasure?" His sword sheared off the rogue's, as once again, he found himself in the clearing on the edge of the swamp.

From high in the trees above them, a raven's scolding caw responded to his question, and he laughed.

"We'll see who laughs last, Riley Sheridan."

"Riley! You have to finish him now!"

He side-stepped the blow the rogue aimed simultaneously

with Lynnette's command, also shouted from somewhere above him. *What the hell?*

The deafening snarls and barks of the dobhar-chù assaulted his hearing as they emerged from the swamp at his back.

"Hurry, Riley! Please!" Lynnette's screams pierced the unholy racket of the otter-dog monsters, and he glanced up at the trees on the edge of the swamp. A massive sea eagle flapping its wings at a raven harrying it caught his attention. He tripped on an upturned rock, fell backward, and landed hard near the first rogue he'd killed. For once, he didn't berate himself for losing his concentration as the third rogue's killing blow thunked uselessly in the soft mud in the space where he'd just stood.

Scrambling to his feet, he wasted no time in finishing off the rogue who desperately worked to free his weapon. It wasn't sporting, but neither were the odds the Morrigan foisted on him. With quick movements, he freed his scabbard from the first dead rogue's back and slid it on over his jacket, momentarily sheathing his claymore inside it before he pulled the man's body next to the other rogue's. Another otter-dog howl rent the stillness of the swamp, setting every hair on his body at attention. He raced up the path to where the headless body of the third rogue lay and dragged it down to lie with the others.

"What are you doing?" Lynnette demanded. Even telepathically, her fear was palpable. *"The dobhar-chùs' lair is in the swamp behind you."*

"This will work. You'll see." He stepped between a pair of trees growing close enough together that he had to stand sideways to fit.

As he made himself small, the rank smell of fish and feces wafted over him, his only warning before the pack of monsters raced past him. The scream of an eagle drew his attention to the trees on the opposite side of the swamp. His heart dropped into his stomach as he watched his talisman fall from the eagle's back.

CHAPTER NINE

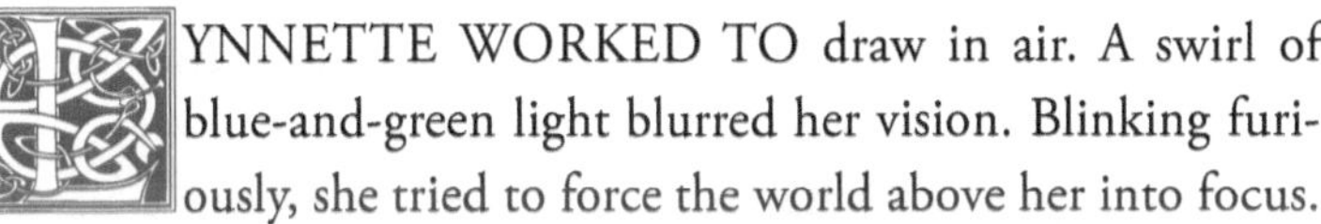

YNNETTE WORKED TO draw in air. A swirl of blue-and-green light blurred her vision. Blinking furiously, she tried to force the world above her into focus. After an age, she could finally discern the trees from the sky. Her shoulder throbbed where it rested atop something hard and unyielding. Hopefully, all she'd have was a bruise. Gingerly, she tried wiggling her toes, which responded, much to her relief. Her left shoulder was on fire, and though she could move her fingers, she couldn't move her arm.

Somewhere overhead, a raven cawed, its call eerie and menacing. It didn't take a genius to know the Morrigan hadn't admitted defeat. Lynnette had no idea whether the war goddess manipulated her symbol, the raven, or had shape-shifted into a raven herself. It didn't matter. The raven harassing Renleigh in her guise as a sea eagle had done its job. Lynnette no longer enjoyed the relative safety of the trees.

Searing pain stabbed her in the back when she sucked in a lungful of air. But that wasn't her problem.

The unearthly snarl of Morgan's chosen monsters forced her to stagger to her feet. While a tree at her back held her upright, nausea threatened to overwhelm her. Her left arm hung uselessly from her shoulder. She hoped it was only a dislocation and not something more serious. Determinedly, she gulped back the remains of her breakfast that threatened a return trip up her esophagus and concentrated on the direction of the sound. In the close confines of the swampy clearing, sound came and went like a hit-and-run, leaving her disoriented.

"Lynnette!"

Even in her thoughts, she could hear Riley's agony as he called her name.

"Lynnette! Answer me. Where are you? How bad are you hurt?"

"My shoulder is sore. But don't worry about me. Worry about taking out the dobhar-chù. There are three of them coming for you. Separate yourself from the dead rogues, and they'll key on the easy prey."

The snap of a twig directly behind her froze her blood. The aroma of decaying fish and other dead things finished what the fall from Renleigh's back from twenty feet in the air started. Against her will, she lost the remnants of her breakfast on the mossy ground in front of her.

Renleigh's voice penetrated her thoughts. *"Whatever you do, don't move."*

Another snapping twig, this one closer, had her clamping a hand over her mouth.

"Morgan has enchanted this place against visualization, so you can't get out of here except by conventional means—or with me," Renleigh communicated. *"When a bear runs past you, don't waste time swinging up on its back."*

She hoped her new friend was in a hurry to shift because the snapping jaws in the forest behind her told her of a nearby dobhar-chù who had an idea a free meal awaited it. In her peripheral vision, a streak of dark fur caught her attention. She hoped it was a bear. In the second it took for the animal to materialize in front of her, her entire life flashed through her mind.

"Get on!"

Renleigh barely slowed as Lynnette grabbed a handful of fur and swung up onto her friend's back. Her shoulder screamed in agony, leaving her with a one-handed hold on her galloping friend. Behind them, a dobhar-chù howled and gnashed its teeth as it chased them through the swamp toward where they'd last seen Riley.

Brackish water splattered over her legs as Renleigh, in grizzly shape, splashed and dashed through the rank-smelling lair of the Morrigan's monsters. Lynnette's shoulder throbbed as she struggled to maintain her hold on her friend. Then Renleigh zigzagged from one tuft of grass-covered boulders to another as they arose in their path, and Lynnette nearly landed in the drink. Before she could question the shaman about what she thought she was doing, she saw that Renleigh had avoided sandwiching them between the three dobhar-chù bearing down on the bodies of the slain rogues and the fourth one currently chasing them.

"Nice work, friend," she communicated as they exited the water and crashed through the trees.

A hair-raising scream pierced the air, drawing her attention back to her warrior. Swiping water and mud from her eyes, she stared in horror at the monster rising on its back legs, its jaws snapping furiously. She couldn't see Riley. Then another scream ripped through the stillness, and the animal crumpled to the ground. The dobhar-chù that had been hot on their tail abruptly changed course, heading straight for where she'd last seen her warrior.

"Slide off and find some cover. I'm going to help your warrior. Make sure he knows I'm on his side."

A surge of anger at her uselessness to both her warrior and her new friend hitched her heart.

"You're not useless. Keep tracking our enemies. Let us know where they are."

Careless of how the foliage tore at her clothes and skin, Lynnette pushed herself toward the interior of a currant bush where she could blend in and watch the action. *"Riley, a grizzly is coming to help you."*

"What the hell?"

"Don't fight her. She's on our side."

The distraction of easy dinner in the form of the dead rogues didn't deter the otter-dog monsters from setting their sights on Riley. Though he'd managed to bring down one of them, its three friends were determined to have him for an appetizer. From her concealed hiding place, she marveled at the strength and cunning of her warrior who feinted and danced in a macabre play with the growling, snapping dobhar-chù. Then one of them apparently had an epiphany and pulled out of the game. To her horror, it slipped into the trees. It's dark fur camouflaged it in the shadows, and it took her several seconds to pick it out from its surroundings.

"Riley! Watch your back! One of the uglies is trying to flank you."

"Don't worry. I'm on it," Renleigh communicated as she crashed through the trees in the monster's wake.

Lynnette had no idea how Renleigh thought she could take on one of Morgan's monsters without a weapon, but she couldn't dwell on it. Instead, she tracked the otter-dog as it slithered and slid on a stealthy roundabout route to cut off Riley's retreat up the trail.

Another otherworldly scream tore the air, swiveling her attention from tracking the third dobhar-chù to the melee of two against one with her warrior. Even from her distant vantage point, she could see the sweat pouring off him as he aimed a killing blow at the animal whose paw he'd severed from its body.

Behind him, Renleigh emerged from the cover of the trees, protecting his back as the third monster attacked him from the front. The downed rogues were now a problem as he had to maneuver around them.

"Step to your right, Riley. There's a hollow behind the big tree. Lure it there, and you gain higher ground."

A nod was his only acknowledgment when he slowly stepped toward the tree.

The fourth monster materialized on the trail and let out a grinding growl that had Lynnette covering the ear she could reach with her functioning hand. It swiped at Renleigh who answered with a low growl of her own. *"Shit. That's gonna leave a mark."* Then the shaman went to town, attacking the dobhar-chù like the crazed mama bear defending her cubs that Lynnette had seen in a nature video once. Her long claws slashed at the monster with blurring speed. It let out a yelp and fell backward. She pounced on it, her deadly bear teeth snapping as she attacked the animal's vulnerable throat.

When the death gurgles of the shaman's victim reached the last monster's ears, it stopped its attack on Riley. Cocking its ears this way and that, it abruptly spun around and raced directly toward her hiding spot. Desperately, she swallowed down the scream clawing at her throat and held her body rigid.

"Bear! It's keyed on Lynnette!" Riley shouted. *"Where are you, sweetheart?"*

It took several seconds for his question to penetrate her terrified brain. *"In the middle of a currant bush on the edge of the water."*

"Don't move!" This from Renleigh.

A crash behind her alerted her that Riley had bent time and space to land near her bushy hiding spot. Renleigh chased after the otter-dog, and Lynnette saw the danger. To skirt her hiding place, her warrior was going to have to slog through the thick mud along the swamp, which gave the monster all the advantage. If he waited for the monster to come to her, he risked sandwiching her between them. She didn't hold out much hope that a currant bush would be sufficient protection against Morgan's creature. Nor did she think it a safe place when her warrior started wielding his claymore. Overhead, the incessantly irritating cawing of a crow mocked their predicament.

Slowly, she lowered herself to a squat, hoping to make herself small enough for her warrior to step over her as he pushed through the bush rather than slogged around it. Right as the monster reached the bush, its putrid breath washing over her and making her gag, it yelped in pain. A bear-sized roar alerted her that Renleigh hadn't wasted any time in coming to her aid. Riley took advantage of the monster's momentary lapse in concentration on her and pushed through the bush, his jeans-clad leg brushing her injured shoulder. She sucked air through clenched teeth and tried to pull herself into a tiny ball with feet.

The dobhar-chù swiped at the bear who batted its claw away. With its attention now fully on the shaman, the otter-dog forgot about the warrior. Riley slammed his sword into the monster's spine—and time slowed to a stop. His claymore was stuck in the monster's body. The monster should have dropped from the mighty blow. Instead, it lashed out with its back feet, catching Riley at the knees and knocking him off balance. It turned and swiped at her warrior, its claws opening a gash across Riley's chest.

Lynnette screamed, and without a thought, jumped to her feet. Crashing through her bushy hiding place, she caught her warrior with her body right before he lost his feet entirely. With her good arm, she pushed against him, keeping him upright.

"Thanks."

He had the audacity to shoot her a cocky smirk over his shoulder.

The monster landed at his feet with an angry bear standing on its back, straddling Riley's sword.

"Good thing I came along when I did, you two," Renleigh growled. "If left to your own devices, I doubt your families would have found enough of you to mourn."

Daintily, she stepped off the dead dobhar-chù and with a mighty shake, transformed back into her human physique. She planted her bare foot on the monster's body and yanked Riley's claymore from its resting place in the creature's spine. Two swipes along the fur cleaned off most of the gore before she handed his weapon back to him.

"Slow down, sister. I took out six rogues and two of these nasty characters by myself, thank-you-very-much."

Renleigh levied a glare at him, but her words were for Lynnette. "The gods saddled you with a cocky one. Looks like you're going to have your hands full."

"Whatever." Riley shot a dirty look in the shaman's direction.

With her shoulder on fire and the aftermath of the battle coursing through her veins, Lynnette was in no mood to listen to the two of them bicker. "This isn't a safe place. It also isn't one we can visualize ourselves out of, apparently. So how 'bout we save the showing off until we're back at the cabin at least."

Though she desperately wanted to hide it, the pain in her shoulder gave itself away. "Lynnette? Sweetheart? Why didn't you say you were hurt?" Riley sheathed his claymore and gingerly smoothed his fingertips up and down her biceps.

"I think I dislocated my shoulder when I fell off Renleigh's back up in the tree." The fear and concern in the depths of his indigo eyes went a long way toward calming her pain. "It's nothing that can't wait until we're out of this godforsaken swamp."

The putrid smell of dead monster threatened to gag her. More than anything, she wanted to remain stoic in front of these two incredibly brave people, which wasn't going to last if they didn't start moving.

Renleigh leveled her a look. "If you pass out before you lead us out of here, it's hard tellin' what nasty surprise Morgan will concoct." Turning her attention to Riley, she said, "You'll have to hold her while I reposition her shoulder. It's not going to be fun, but you'll feel a lot better after, I promise," she added for Lynnette's benefit. "Come on."

"Come on, Sunshine. Let's get you fixed up so we can get out of here." With great care, he positioned her good arm over his shoulders and slipped his arm across her back. Then he bent and slipped his other arm behind her knees and lifted her to his chest.

Squeezing her eyes closed, she hissed in a breath of pain.

"I'm sorry, Lynnette."

The worry in his eyes nearly undid her. "We're good. It could be so much worse." She attempted a weak smile, one he clearly didn't buy as he wasted no time stepping over the downed dobhar-chù and all but running to catch up to Renleigh.

When they reached a wide spot on the trail, he slowly lowered her to her feet. The grave expression on her new friend's face mirrored on her warrior's told her she wasn't going to enjoy what happened next. *Like anything that happened after breakfast was fun,* she thought ruefully.

"I'll make it up to you. Promise." Riley waggled his brows, and she shook her head. Cocky didn't begin to describe this man.

Then again, visions of the previous night and the early morning flitted through her head, leaving her core heavy and taking her mind off the fiery throbbing in her shoulder.

That's when Renleigh moved. Grabbing Lynnette's wrist with one hand and her bicep with the other, she tugged hard. Simultaneously, Riley barred his arm across her chest, his other arm wrapped around her waist. The gunshot sound of her shoulder popping back into place startled her. For a second, her body floated before another uncontrollable bout of nausea leveled her. Apparently, the other two expected it because they let go of her immediately, and she stumbled two steps to the bushes. She thought she would have felt better if she'd had something left to expel instead of dry heaving in the most unladylike manner imaginable. Without thinking, she swiped her left forearm over her mouth then stared at her raised limb. While the throbbing in her shoulder had settled down to a dull roar, at least her arm was functional again.

Riley's steady hand at the base of her spine warmed her even through the mortification of him seeing her like this.

"Nothing to be ashamed of, babe. Everyone loses their lunch at least once when they go into battle." His reassuring smile dropped a notch when Renleigh joined them. "Right, shaman?"

"My name is Renleigh Rogan." She extended her hand to him.

He shook it. "Riley Sheridan. Thanks for helping us."

"Yeah, well, like I said, we'd better not waste anymore time in this hellhole. Morgan doesn't need incentive to come after us again. May I have what's left of your T-shirt to make a sling for your talisman?"

Without hesitation, Riley shucked his leather jacket and scabbard then tugged his shirt over his head. Lynnette gasped when she saw the four nasty gashes that marred the perfection of his sculpted chest. Like they were no big deal, he shrugged and handed his ragged shirt to the shaman. While he slipped his sword and scabbard and leather jacket back on, Renleigh deftly fashioned his T-shirt into a sling that she delicately dropped over Lynnette's head and threaded her arm into. Lynnette sighed in immediate relief.

The shaman nodded in satisfaction at her handiwork then caught Lynnette's eye. "Lead the way."

Ankle-turning rocks littered the uneven path, some slick and round, others jagged and sharp. The rocks only gave way when gnarly roots bisected the path, which meant they had to pick their way along rather than hike out at speed. Where the path paralleled the stream flowing out of the swamp, another path emerged a few steps higher toward the mountainside. When Riley chose that path to walk beside her, Lynnette stopped.

"Backtrack onto this one, please."

He tipped his head, a mocking expression marring his handsome features. "I can't just hop over to you?" The distance was less than a yard, something he could easily traverse in one stride.

"Not if you want to leave this place."

He exchanged a look with the shaman whose raised brow was her only response.

Blowing out an exasperated sigh, he said, "Fine," and sauntered back to where the two trails merged. Renleigh picked her way back to meet him, chanting something Lynnette couldn't hear over the creek burbling alongside them. Then the two of them fell back in behind her, and they continued their journey to the roadway.

When they reached the road, Riley fell into step beside her.

"What was that back there? On the trail?" He reached for her good hand, lacing his fingers through hers, his touch zapping an electric current through her blood.

"It turns out, we discovered my skill."

Abruptly, he stopped and tugged her around to face him.

"When all the noise of battle silenced, I crawled out of the back of your Jeep. I saw your tracks that glowed with blue-green iridescence and followed them back around the cabin to the drop-off behind it." She glanced at Renleigh who waited a little ahead of them. "A bear showed up"—she laughed—"and gave me some better options for following your tracks, tracks she couldn't see in any of her guises."

She squeezed his hand, the side of her mouth curving up. "No matter where you go, I'll always be able to find you."

When Riley leaned in for a kiss, Renleigh interrupted with a loud throat clearing. "Trackers have other skills as well. The two of you should probably use somewhere enchanted against Morgan's interference rather than this civilian hunting cabin to discover exactly what Lynnette's are." She motioned for them to keep walking, and they fell into step behind her.

Riley shot the shaman a look that could have singed paint off a wall, not that she paid the least attention as she continued walking toward the cabin. With a petulant-sounding sigh, he started walking, Lynnette's hand still firmly clasped in his as she walked beside him.

CHAPTER TEN

HE CLOSER THEY drove to his parents' compound on the Flathead Lake side of the mountain, the more Riley's nerves churned in his gut. Teasing from his dad and brothers he could handle. Disappointment from his mom when she found out what he'd attempted? Not so much. Plus, his chest burned like fire ants feasted on his flesh. He hoped their neighbor and friend Siobhan Lochlann had some druidic magic for dobhar-chù gashes.

Beside him, his talisman sat still as a stone, and he wondered about her level of pain. Falling off an eagle's back and dropping twenty feet to land on an exposed root probably should have killed her instead of merely dislocating her shoulder. The thought had his chest burning for a completely different reason. His cockiness hadn't only put his own life in danger—he could have lost his talisman before he even had the chance to explore all their promising possibilities.

His mom had never sustained any serious injury that he'd ever seen, so he didn't have a clue if talismans had the same or similar supernatural healing capabilities as warriors, but when he sneaked a glance at Lynnette's stunning profile and the pain thinning her plump lips, he certainly hoped so. Being the cause of his mate's agony pricked his conscience even more than facing his mom's displeasure.

They hung a left off the narrow highway onto a dirt two-track that climbed up the mountainside to his parents' home. Sensing his talisman's heightened discomfort, he shifted gears and pushed his Jeep a little harder. Reaching across her body, she covered his hand on the gearshift and squeezed. Hard.

"What?" he asked, his voice low.

"Before Renleigh and I left the cabin, I tried to reach out to your twin."

Involuntarily, he eased his foot off the gas.

"He didn't respond." Her eyes found his when he glanced away from the road. "Why would he not respond? Is your family even going to like me?"

Riley flipped his hand over, cuffing her palm in his. "Knowing my brother, he had his shield firmly in place because he didn't want to hear me gloat about being the first to find my talisman."

A sharp curve demanded his attention, and he let her go to steer around it.

"You would gloat about that?"

"Obviously, you don't have brothers." A laugh escaped him. "Hell yes I would—and will—gloat about being the first one to find my mate. Especially after the way the gods favored me." He didn't even try to stop the smirk that sprang to his lips. "Have you even seen you?"

She slid down in her seat. "How can you say that when you watched me lose what was left of my breakfast back there?"

"Sunshine, you were incredible in that swamp. A real champ. I doubt there's a warrior alive who wouldn't have lost his stomach after having his shoulder reset the way Renleigh popped yours." His palm found the smooth skin where her short skirt rode up her thigh, and he tested the silky texture with his fingertips. "My family is going to be all kinds of impressed with your toughness and your quick-witted insights into getting us out of the scrape I got us into."

Yeah, he needed to own his mistake, not only with his family, but especially with his lady.

"I could have suggested the guesthouse on my parents' property. But I wanted privacy too, Riley," she whispered.

He gave her thigh a tiny squeeze and let a grin tug at the corner of his mouth. "So I'm not the only daredevil in this duo. Good to know."

The Sheridan compound came into view, and Riley maneuvered around the left side of the house to the long garage in the back. Hitting the button on the ceiling of his ride, he activated the garage door of the bay assigned to him and drove in, hitting the button a second time to close the door. He cut the engine and turned in his seat. Because he couldn't seem to stop touching her, he cupped Lynnette's jaw, his work-roughened thumb caressing the skin over her high cheekbone. "My family is going to love you. Not only because you're the key to making me a whole warrior but also because you're intelligent, a little snarky, and a whole lot tough." He leaned across the center console. "The added bonus for me is that you're gorgeous, inside and out," he said against her lips as he brushed a kiss over them.

The dreamy expression on her face when he pulled away was short-lived. "We've barely known each other a weekend. So I'm not sure all your observations are accurate."

"I've seen you in action, babe. You're the real deal." Liking her dreamy expression better—especially because he knew he'd put it on her face—he leaned in and kissed her again, a gentle pressure with a promise of more.

When he pulled away this time, the softness in her eyes conveyed a completely different response, one he wanted to take his time exploring in great detail.

"Let's get the introductions over and see if our druid friend has some magic cures for our battle wounds." In one lithe movement, he opened the door and stepped out of his Jeep. Bending time and space, he opened Lynnette's door right as she reached for the handle. Sweeping his hand out in a grand gesture, he said, "My lady. After you."

He worried she might have strained her expressive moss-green eyes with the epic eye roll she gifted him, but he caught the ghost of a smile on her lips as she stepped past him to the door leading out of the garage. When they entered the house through the mudroom, they could hear the low rumble of his brothers in some sort of argument in the kitchen, one they interrupted when they stepped through the door.

"Look what the cat dragged in," his oldest brother Rowan began before he noticed the state of Riley's chest. "Whoa, man. Did you get in a fight with a mountain lion?"

"Worse. Dobhar-chù."

"What the hell?" This from Rio who stood from his seat in the breakfast nook opposite Rowan.

"But that's not important. Can one of you call Siobhan, see if she can come over to help my talisman?" Side-stepping to reveal his mate, he said, "Rio, you remember Lynnette from the Lammas Eve bonfire the other night? Rowan, this is Lynnette Montgomery. My talisman." He didn't even bother to keep the pride from his voice.

"Did you try to reach out to me sometime early this morning?" Rio asked, his eyes laser-focused on Lynnette.

Her chin went up. "Yes. Riley was in trouble, and I thought you could help, but you didn't respond."

Riley cocked a brow at his twin who shifted his weight from foot to foot.

"I thought I was dreaming." A red tinge crept along Rio's cheekbones. "I might have taken the party too far last night."

Riley exchanged a glance with Rowan. This was new. Rio never stepped out of line. Ever.

"Doesn't matter now. But as you can see, we could use the services of a healer." Riley's tone was as dry as sand.

"I thought I heard your voice," his mom said as she breezed into the kitchen from the direction of the living room, Siobhan Lochlann following close behind. Thank the gods. Beside him, he could sense his talisman's stores of energy flagging after the way their day had begun. Glancing out the window at the shadows of the forest surrounding the house, he thought it was close to dinnertime. The growling of his stomach confirmed it. After the day they'd had, it was a wonder either of them was still standing upright.

"Mom! Hey. Um—"

"Riley Sean Sheridan. What have you done to your chest?" In her motherly concern for his welfare, she'd somehow completely missed the stunning woman standing next to him.

"Siobhan can see to that in a minute. First, I'd like to introduce you to Lynnette Montgomery—my talisman—who could use Siobhan's skills first."

His mother's shriek of delighted surprise nearly split every eardrum in the room. "Riley! Your talisman! Oh, my darling son." She hugged him hard, reigniting the fires on his chest that had banked themselves in his consciousness while he talked to his brothers. "Lynnette! Oh!" Beside him, his talisman hissed in a pained breath, and his mom at last paid attention to their injuries. "You're hurt. Both of you. What happened?" Tossing her hands in the air, her standard response to any dustup he and his brothers ever got into, she said, "You can tell us as we patch you up. Siobhan, this is Lynnette, Riley's talisman." His mother's introduction sounded like she'd known Lynnette for ages rather than having just met her. A tiny grin ghosted Siobhan's mouth as she nodded at Lynnette. "From the looks of things, we should start with her."

⟊

"Dumb-ass move, bro. How the hell did you think you'd escape Morgan's notice, training with your talisman out in the open like that?" Rio asked as they tucked into steaming bowls of beef stew their father set in front of them.

After Siobhan had tended to their wounds, they joined the others for dinner Owen cooked. Riley's dad ladled another bowl from a pot in the middle of the dining room table and handed it to Rio, an arched tilt to his brow, which Rio ignored.

Leaning close to Lynnette, Riley whispered in her ear, "Dad's the cook around here, in case you hadn't figured that out. Lucky for us, I'm more like him than our mom who can only cook breakfast."

She shot him a side-eye, while on his other side, his twin cuffed the side of his head.

"Hey, knock it off."

"Answer the question."

"Because I didn't want to deal with my brothers during my private time and training with my lady." He gifted Lynnette one of his signature smirks then turned and cuffed his brother back. "And you're acting exactly the way I expected you would."

"Boys—" their dad cleared his throat. "Gentlemen. This is not the time or the place."

The cobalt blue of their dad's eyes intensified almost to black, which was enough for both of them to remember themselves.

"I'm sorry, Sunshine. It's going to take time to get used to my changed circumstances." Under the table, he gave his talisman's thigh a gentle squeeze and worked to keep the smirk off his face when she clamped her thighs together at his light touch. Turning his attention back to his brother, he said, "I might be the youngest of us three, but I'm the one who grew up the fastest."

"Uh-huh. That was one grown-up decision you made to train

without the protections of druidic enchantments," Rowan said from across the table. His eyes danced as he shoved food into his mouth.

"We'll see to your privacy, Riley," Sian said from her spot at the opposite end of the table from his dad. "Those healing chants and special herbs Siobhan used should make bonding and training much more comfortable in short order."

Riley knew better than to trust his mom's matter-of-fact tone. Sure enough, when he glanced over at her, he caught her winking at his dad. He swore his parents had been on a honeymoon from the minute his dad discovered his mom to be his talisman. If anything, their youngest son discovering his talisman only intensified their bond.

A thought struck him. With Lynnette, he could have what his parents had. Though rare in the warrior community, there were instances of talismans and warriors not fully bonding. But his parents' example made him think he and Lynnette had a better-than-even chance at living the rest of their lives as one long honeymoon. He hid a smile and scratched at his chest where Siobhan's poultice worked on his wounds. That is, they had a chance at a honeymoon life when they weren't taking on Morgan and her minions.

"While your dad was cooking this deliciousness"—Sian saluted Owen with her raised spoon—"Siobhan chanted some special spells over the guesthouse, Riley. It's all yours and Lynnette's for as long as you need."

"Don't take advantage of that, little bro," Rowan warned. "I'm only willing to take up *some* of your slack at work." His genuine smile belied his words and warmed Riley's heart.

Beside him, Rio said, "Ditto." He directed his gaze at his food, but Riley knew his twin well. His brothers had his back and would give him the time he needed to bond with Lynnette.

"Glad that's settled," he said as he dropped his spoon in his empty bowl. "If it's all the same to you, we'll take our dessert out to the guesthouse."

"Thought you might want to do that. I set aside some chocolate mousse pie in a container on the counter. There's a pint of vanilla-caramel ice cream in the freezer in the mudroom." Though Owen didn't look up from his meal, mirth danced over his lips, Riley's cue to take off before the relentless teasing had a chance to begin.

"You ready, Sunshine?"

Lynnette had remained so quiet during the meal, he worried she was having second thoughts about bonding with him. From the corner of his eye, he sneaked a glance her way. But the pretty shade of pink sneaking across her cheekbones gave him an entirely different idea. He stood and pushed his chair in, then helped Lynnette from her chair. When she reached for her place setting, he waved her off, gathering up their bowls and utensils and leading her out of the dining room. After he put their dishes into the dishwasher, he grabbed the dessert his dad had mentioned and led his talisman out the back door and across the yard to the guesthouse tucked into a small clearing in the trees east of the garage.

His hands full, he motioned to the heavy pine door. "Go on in."

With a tiny nod, she walked into the cabin ahead of him. After he set their treats on the counter of the kitchenette, he turned the lock on the door. Crossing her free arm over her injured one still in a sling, she lifted a brow and waited.

"They'll leave us alone here." In his mind, he crossed his fingers. "But in case they decide to 'check on us,'" he added with air quotes "I want them to know we can take care of ourselves just fine."

"That was awkward."

"I think meeting the parents for the first time usually is.

Doubly so for our community." With a smile, he snagged her hand and brushed a kiss over her knuckles. "I'll get my turn with your parents soon enough."

She relaxed for the first time since they sat down to dinner with his family.

Careful of her injury, he pulled her into his arms. "We truly are safe here, Lynnette." He rubbed his nose along hers and rested his forehead against hers, closing his eyes and breathing her in. "We can take our time, get to know each other—well." He let his smile loose, the one he saved especially for her. "And we can work on all the nuances of your special skill in the safety of our training room."

"Your parents are deeply in love."

"They are. From the way they tell it, from the first time they bonded, they had all the feelings for each other."

Clearing her throat, she caught and held his eyes. "I want that."

Holding her face in his hands, he returned her stare. "I want that, too." He brushed his lips over hers, a soft enticement she mimicked, then added pressure. A smile stretched over his mouth, and he slipped his tongue out to taste her lips. Again, she mimicked him with her own little grin against his skin and plunged her tongue inside his mouth. It was a dare he could never in a million lifetimes refuse.

When her luscious rack pressed into his chest, the poultice shifted, causing an itch he couldn't ignore. Panting with the need her kisses had incited in him from the very first one, he said, "I need a shower. Want to join me?"

A slow smile spread over her features. "You wash my back and I wash yours?"

"I was thinking chests, but we can start with backs."

Her melodic laughter was a sound he wanted to hear over and over.

"I could use a shower."

CHAPTER ELEVEN

LONG TIME LATER, sated and out of hot water, they stepped from the shower, their laughter ringing over the tiled walls of the bathroom. "Are we going to try that again, sometime?" Lynnette asked.

"I certainly hope so. Only somewhere with a bigger hot water heater." Riley sighed. Gently, he ran the fluffy bath towel over her skin. "You sure your shoulder isn't giving you pain?"

She blinked up at him in surprise. "I didn't notice it at all."

"Told you Siobhan would fix you up."

Lightly, she dragged her fingertip over the thin pink lines that were all that was left of the deep gashes from his battle with the dobhar-chù. "Good thing you have supernatural healing ability, Riley Sean Sheridan."

Wrapping his arms around her, he said, "You know my mom only uses all three of my names when she's exasperated with me."

"I caught that, yes."

"Even after that"—he nodded toward the shower—"you're saying you're exasperated with me?" he teased.

She leaned in and kissed the widest scar. "I've never been so afraid in my life, Riley. We'd only just found each other. I know we're lucky that happened so early in our lives, but after one night with you, I couldn't imagine my life without you." She kissed his chest again. "But Morgan could have so easily ensured that I had a front row seat to the end of that life."

He gifted her his cockiest grin. "You're bonded to a Sheridan. It's going to take more than some otter-dog monsters to take me out." Sobering, he stared deep into her eyes. "The gods intend for bonded warrior pairs to love each other. It's why the bonding ritual unites us physically. But even beyond the incredible sex—"

"Incredible, huh? With my lack of experience?" She winked, but he heard her worry in the question.

"Even beyond the stupidly fantastic sex"—his lips curved up—"I would have fallen for you. If you'd have seen you in the firelight at the Lammas Eve bonfire, you would have been half in love with you too." He brushed another kiss over her mouth. "In case you haven't figured it out yet, the honeymoon has already started." Sliding a hand over her lush backside, he pulled her tighter against him, letting her feel what her nearness did to him. The moss-green of her eyes intensified, and she let out a tiny sigh that nearly undid him. "Glad to know we're on the same page."

A shriek of laughter escaped her as he scooped her high into his arms and carried her to the king-size bed in the middle of the adjoining bedroom. Taking care with her shoulder, he laid her on her back and climbed over her, kissing those plump lips he knew would haunt his dreams for the rest of his life. While his mouth was busy with hers, he let his hands explore the full mounds of her breasts. Beneath him, she writhed and arched, seeking more of his touch, and he chuckled low in his throat.

Her erect nipples teased the palms of his hands, enticing him to kiss them. Lynnette's cries of pleasure at his tongue laving and sucking the turgid tips spurred him on. Gliding a hand down her body, he teased his fingertips over the sensitive skin of her belly, enjoying the goose bumps that sprang up at his touch. When he slipped his fingers through the curls at the jointure of her thighs, her legs parted sweetly, allowing him to test her readiness for him.

Slick wetness and a swollen clit greeted his touch, and he pushed up on his knees. He'd wanted her again almost from the second he came down from the orgasm she'd given him in the shower. When she reached for him, pumping his erection with her smooth, warm palm, he gritted his teeth and tightened his ass cheeks to keep from surging into her. She stared up at him from beneath hooded lids, her eyes glittering in challenge, and he gave in. In one smooth stroke, he joined them together. As the slick, velvety walls of her pussy pulsed around him, he fisted the sheets on either side of her shoulders and willed himself to hold back from pounding hard into her as his body demanded.

Lynnette wasn't idle. She feathered her fingertips over the healing scars on his chest, up over his shoulders, and along his traps. With insistent pressure, she pulled him down for a kiss that turned his blood to molten lava. She gave him no choice but to move, setting a rhythm with her lips and tongue that their bodies mimicked in love's oldest dance.

When he couldn't take any more, he pounded into her. She lifted her hips, meeting his thrusts, her moans and whimpers morphing into breathy sighs of "Yes! Yes! More! Yes!" before her back arched, her chin aimed at the ceiling, and her eyelids fluttered closed. His name on her lips sounded like a prayer before his own orgasm barreled down his spine and he shouted her name loud enough to be heard the next county over.

Afterward, he pulled the covers over them and tucked her into his side. His throat raw, he spoke softly in the quiet dark of the falling evening. "I know we're young, and we both have to finish school and training with each other and building ourselves as a fighting unit for Scathach and the warrior community. . ."

She nodded against his chest.

"And we've only known each other for a weekend. But what do you say to a short engagement?"

For several long minutes, she remained quiet, tracing her fingers over the skin of his chest. At last, she said, "The gods determined we should be together, and they didn't waste time letting us find each other. We should probably honor their intentions and not waste time preparing for the inevitable."

Until it whooshed out of him in a harsh laugh, he hadn't realized he held his breath at her answer. Tipping his head up to look into the endless green of her eyes, he asked, "Are you always this romantic?"

The side of her mouth came up in wry twist. "In the short time we've known each other, I've discovered that you tend to jump first and think about it later." Her eyes stayed on his as she kissed the side of his chest. "Lucky for us, I'm practical." She winked. "But you can let your inner romantic go nuts when you officially propose."

A slow smile tugged at his lips. "Challenge accepted."

If you want more of Riley and Lynnette's story, let me know. I have ideas. ;)

If this is your first experience with the *Talisman Series*, the next six books are waiting for you. The seventh book is coming in summer 2023. See what happens when a rogue warrior runs into a shape-shifting shaman strong enough to take him on. Jaime Lennox's test is Renleigh Rogan, and their story is going to be a wild one.

You can find out more about what is coming in the *Talisman Series* and in my rock star romance *Balefire Series* as well as what is happening with my sports romance *Match Play* by subscribing to my newsletter at https://www.tamderudderjackson.com. You can also reach out to me on social media @tamstales32 on Instagram or at Tam's Romance Warriors on Facebook.

Reviews help me reach more readers, so if you enjoyed this novella, please take a minute to leave a review on whatever platforms work for you. I appreciate it. Thanks!

ACKNOWLEDGMENTS

Thank you to all the readers of the *Talisman Series* who wanted to know more about Riley and Lynnette. This novella exists because of you. Writing this one also gave me a great excuse to go poking around in Celtic mythology for new monsters and bad situations, which are catnip for this writer wanting to put her characters through the wringer. ;)

A huge thanks to my editor. I couldn't do this without you, Nikki Busch. It's hard to believe this is the eleventh book we've worked on together, and with every one, you make me a better writer. I hope our editing partnership goes on and on.

Special thanks to my critique partners: LindaRae Sande, KJ Gillenwater, Sara Vinduska, and Jacque Coburn. Your encouragement and comments on the early draft made this a better story. You all teach me so much about how to pursue this writing career better. Thanks for all the fun at our bi-monthly dinners.

Another special thanks goes to my PA Julia Goldhirsh who works tirelessly to help me put my books in front of more readers. Your ideas and enthusiasm continue to inspire me.

Finally, the reviewers, bloggers, and fellow authors who read and review my books are so important to me. Thanks a bunch for your time and support of my writing and for helping me reach new audiences.

ABOUT THE AUTHOR

Like the tagline of her first novel, Tam DeRudder Jackson's personal motto is "Love is worth the risk." Readers and reviewers have praised her stories for her swoon-worthy characters, movie-quality world building, and strong writing. Though she's a voracious reader of all genres of romance, her favorite genres to write are paranormal and contemporary. When she's not writing or reading, she's probably traveling or skiing or dancing at a rock concert.